I0763583

Inside the Playhouse:
Tales, Teasers & Temptations

Kay Taylor

Inside the Playhouse: Tales, Teasers & Temptations

For inquiries, permissions, or collaborations, contact:

ktaylor@playhouseplaythings.com

First edition

ISBN: 979-8-218-45058-8

Printed in the United States of America

Disclaimer

This book contains explicit erotic content that explores themes of intimacy, desire and sensuality. While we strive to provide a diverse and compelling range of narratives, some readers may find certain scenes or themes triggering or uncomfortable.

Please be advised that the content within may include depictions of sensitive topics such as BDSM, ENM, power dynamics, and explicit sexual encounters. These themes are presented within the context of adult fiction and are intended for mature audiences only.

Reader discretion is strongly advised. If you are sensitive to explicit content or find certain themes distressing, we recommend exercising caution or selecting alternative reading material.

Additionally, it is important to prioritize your emotional well-being while engaging with this book. Should you find any content distressing or triggering, we encourage you to seek support from loved ones or professional resources.

Thank you for your understanding and discretion.

Introduction

Inside the Playhouse: Tales, Teasers & Temptations is no ordinary book – it's a seduction waiting to happen. Step through the velvet-draped doorway and into a world where curiosity is celebrated, pleasure is worshipped, and nothing is off-limits.

These pages don't whisper; they moan and beg to be touched. Inside, you'll find a collection of short stories that burn slow and hot – some playful, some wicked, all deliciously indulgent. Each tale is a brush against bare skin, a gasp in the dark, a bold exploration of what happens when desire is given room to breathe...and bite.

But this isn't just about voyeurism – it's about you. Between stories, you'll find journal prompts that dare you to look inward, to tease out your fantasies, confessions, and cravings. They aren't sweet little reflections- they're raw, intimate invitations to undress your mind and surrender to the truth of what turns you on.

To tempt you further, provocative images created by the incredibly gifted @RisenFromRuins are woven throughout the experience – sultry visuals that don't just complement the stories but heighten them. They seduce the eye and linger in the imagination, pulling you deeper into the Playhouse with every glance.

This is your playground of passion, your private stage of exploration. Inside the Playhouse celebrates the art of arousal, the beauty of bold desire, and the thrill of letting go – without apology.

So go ahead. Turn the page. Let the words wrap around your body like silk, let the images kiss your thoughts, and let the prompts pull you under. You're not just reading this – you're feeling it. And once you're inside the Playhouse...leaving is the last thing you'll want to do.

Part One

Soft Fire

It's About You

This is your permission slip to imagine boldly, desire freely, and claim the sensual life you crave. No filters, no shame – just you, your fantasies, and the freedom to explore what truly turns you on. Describe, in vivid detail, what your ideal sex life looks and feels like. Who are you when you're deeply in tune with your desires? What does pleasure look like in your world?

Erogenous Zones

Go beyond the typical areas like the thighs, ears, and neck. Check off the areas that make your body tingle or add any you find that are specifically pleasing.

- o Scalp
- o Behind the Ears
- o Temples
- o Jawline & Chin
- o Eyes/Under Eyes
- o Lips
- o Clavicle/Collarbone
- o Inner Arms (Biceps or Elbow Crease)
- o Underarms
- o Side of Torso/Ribcage
- o Small of the Back
- o Palms
- o Webbing Between Fingers
- o Inner Wrists

- o Back of Knees
- o Ankles
- o Arch of Foot
- o Toes & Toe Webbings
- o Under the Chest/Breast
- o Sternum
- o Lower Belly
- o Spine
- o Shoulder Blades
- o Gluteal Crease (Under the buttock

Any other areas come to mind? List them below.

____

____

____

____

____

____

____

____

____

Fantasy Land

What are the thoughts that reside in the depths of your mind? The ones that creep in when the world is quiet, when your fingers hover just above forbidden places, aching to trace fantasies you've never dared to say out loud?

Do you covet celestial worship? Are you a fiend for lawless degradation? Or are you a switch?

All the above? Or something beyond?

The more your appetite is repressed, the more you yearn to satiate the craving. Until all the repressed desire gathers, and it demands a voice. It demands release. And we could release it together.

Step into my endless mind and see what I don't show. A wondrous place where pleasure knows no bounds. One where fantasy dances on the line of reality and all your dreams can come true.

In my land, I'm allowed more than one. Dare I say a plethora. Each body succumbing to my desires. Each hand tracing my arches so gently. Teasing tastes of flesh as they massage me, melting away my stresses and inhibitions. One would spread me while the other would enter. Another face to face, exchanging heavy breaths in sync with the strokes of their partner. Our bodies dancing with one another; with mine at the center of devotion. Firm grips on my neck and hips take me deeper into wonderland. Kisses on my thighs and lips edge me into my peak. Lust having its way with each of us. We become a single entity linked by a burning passion and I am boundless. Serve me, I am your majesty.

Other times, I'd rather be bad. Really bad. I choose to submit everything to you. And you take me. Take me lower than ever before and I give you all my praises. Explore your most wicked whims with me as your vessel. My master, your presence emanating pure power. Grab me by the neck so I feel the pressure of your fingertips marking my throat. Bend my will. Speak to me. Curse my name and tell me the worst to make me feel the best. Handle me. I feel your fury in every impact against my skin, and I love it. Give me all your pain and danger as a keepsake and make it last. Go beyond what is admissible. Shower me in your rain and ignominy as I beg you "please...more".

But sharing is caring, of course. And my capabilities extend further than you could imagine. What if we switched the roles? You don't know how much power it gives me. And still just a glimpse into your world. Get on your knees. French kiss every inch until you are drowning in me. Your tongue dancing inside and around my best parts. I want you to struggle to breathe. Dedicate your every living second to my sole pleasure until my knees tremble in your grasp. But not so fast. Tell me you don't mind if I went inside. Bend over, now. I promise to be gentle. The feel of the masculine frame at my fingertips feeds my insatiable appetite, but just a little. I want to feel you, inside and out. Make me proud and stay just like that.

Good boy.

Let's take a break for now.

Tell me how you feel. I can still sense the tingling on my skin. The acts I dream of fuel me to explore and I think you should join me. I've shown you my realm, now show me yours. It can't be much messier than mine, can it?

To My Dearest Friend:

I remember you so gentle and gracious.

Illuminating every corridor with a presence that penetrated my every sense. You were impossible to neglect, and we became inseparable.

Our contradictions interlocked like a puzzle, what seemed a perfect match. And you've always provoked my imagination. Still as pure as the day we met.

What if I told you...

That I love you?

That I want to be your first?

Would you abide? I want to learn your body in ways you've yet to think about. Teach you how to indulge in pleasure and taste your first transcendence.

Let me rest my cheek inside your thigh.

Relax...and let my lips meet yours. You're soft, delicate in the way of a white rose. With a nectar sweeter than honey. Skin smooth like porcelain. An aroma of overwhelming desire.

Soft French kisses to welcome my love.

My tongue dancing in your pool of moisture. I can feel your satisfaction through your fingertips on my neck. Your soft gasps just plunge me deeper.

My fingers trace your sex in the most tender manner, admiring your essence. I enter your warmth gently, letting you take in each moment of bliss as I drown in your water. Relax your head back and drift into ecstasy. Tell me when you're ready.

You've never felt this before.

Your legs tighten around me. My breath against your center, I whisper "Breathe." Your exhales tremble in sync with your body. "Please..." You beg for me in a way like never before. I carry you into euphoria.

You taste yourself on my lips for the first time.

You make it hard not to have seconds.

I'll let you rest. You've honored me with irreplaceable enchantment. One with magic of a million charmers. Yet, I'm simply living in my dreams.

And we are platonic.

Your virtue remains and I indulge from afar. But what if...

What if I told you that I love you?

Grip me like you own me
Leave markings on my skin

Choke me with your right hand
Tease my pussy with your left

"You're getting wetter"

Slide your tongue around my neck
Bite me just hard enough

"Fuck.... Yes"

Play in my fountain
Have all the fun

"Please...Slide your fingers in me
Stroke me slow"

"Just like this?"

Just like that
Keep the same pressure

Roll my nipples between your fingers
Look me in the eye and bite your lip

"Faster"

Hold onto me tightly
Talk to me nicely

"That's my good girl"
"I feel it coming. Go on, you can do it"

Don't change a thing
Carry me through
Take control of me
I'm almost there...

"Oh my God!"
"Yes! Yes! Please...don't stop. Fuck! I'm cu...

The Little Things

Sex is seldom about penetration alone. A lot of times it's the little things that *really* get us off. How you're touched and kissed. The subtle looks with hidden meanings. A specific tone of voice. Use this space to name some, or all the small nuances that get you going the most.

His 5 Languages

Words of Affirmation:

"You know, you mean the world to me."

His rich baritone voice has a way of bringing peace and pleasure to my body and my mind. Smooth and sultry but with just enough grit to make anyone bend to his will. There is always such power in his voice. He knows just how weak his words make me and cannot help but use his tongue to his advantage. The way he commands me is like no other and he makes me wet with each word he speaks.

"Take off your clothes. Get on your knees. I want to see how lovely you look waiting to please me."

My mouth is salivating looking up at him. Patiently awaiting his approval and I am throbbing. With a single nod of his head, I take him in as much as I can. I'm thinking about edging myself from the way he moans with satisfaction.

"Fuck. Yes, baby. That's my girl. Go deeper."

His girl, his princess, baby doll. I love the way he encourages me, and it is nearly impossible to suppress the urge to please him. I obey his demands and proceed to swallow him whole. I'm gagging looking into his eyes, but I know he loves my dedication and the sound of me suffocating from his girth. I'm dripping watching him lose himself in my mouth. The feeling of his hardness against my tongue has my clit twitching. Before I can reach down to satisfy myself, I feel his gentle touch on my cheek.

"Are you ready for me to fuck that pretty pierced pussy? Lay down there and do not move."

Physical Touch:

His hands are almost double the size of mine. Strong but he has a touch with the perfect balance of dominance and tenderness. I feel his fingers gliding up the inside of my thighs as I lay on the bed. With a firm squeeze, he slowly spreads my legs apart to see all my beauty. I watch him admire me as he licks his lips. He raises my leg and begins kissing me softly from my ankle to my inner thigh and rests his thumbs against my folds with his fingertips digging into my hips. He begins to use my wetness to tease me, sliding his hands all around my pussy. Eyes closed and enjoying my treatment, I feel one of his hands come around my back as he applies pressure down my spine, releasing all my tensions. A slight moan escapes my lips, and he knows exactly what he is doing to me. I arch my body closer to his as he controls it like a joystick. His teasing turns into full-on pleasure as he quickens his rhythm and places a finger at the entrance of me as if to say he's ready to explore further. I hold his hand in place and grind myself into his palm, trying to maintain my control for as long as he will let me. I want more just as he does. I slowly push his waiting finger inside of me and he begins thrusting in and out at just the perfect pace to make me come effortlessly. But will he let me? He knows I can barely stand the thought of being deprived of release. As if he has read my mind, he tells me to keep still, and I comply. He then adds a second finger and curls his fingertips to massage the soft, wet walls of my insides as I squirm in his hands, quickly disobeying his command. He leans toward me to marry his lips to my chest. Placing on me soft kisses joined by his wet tongue, tracing the contours of my breasts while he fingers me into ecstasy. I think he senses that I am nearing the edge, so he slowly pulls his hands away from me. I look at him with both slight regret and instant relief as I am not quite ready to finish.

"Get up. Come with me. I have something for you."

I clumsily rise to my feet as I try to regain stability in my legs. I am not sure what he has planned but I am anxious to find out.

Acts of Service:

Following him to our master bathroom, I can smell the distinct fragrance of florals and sandalwood. As we enter, I notice candles have been lit and there is a trail of rose petals leading to the tub that is filled with a light mist of bubbles. I turn to him and give him a look of wonderment.

Coming up behind me, I feel his arms wrap around my body as he brings me closer to his.

"I want to make you feel special tonight. You deserve everything I'm going to give you."

With both hands on my waist, he guides me to the tub and helps me settle in. The water is the perfect temperature, but my insides are burning with desire for him, more each minute.

"Close your eyes and relax."

I lay my head back on the edge and breathe deep as he begins massaging my neck and chest, his breath smooth and heavy in my ear just outside the tub. Every muscle begins to unwind as his hands and words soothe me. He whispers the most tender words of love in my ear, and it makes my pussy flutter. His touch grows firmer as he explores my body beneath the surface. Dancing around my nipples and stroking my hips before finally meeting my clit again. His fingers make tiny circles around my pearl and lap wave upon wave of ecstasy against me. Water continues to splash out of the tub and onto our stone floors as I struggle to keep still. He cannot keep his hands off me and I am enjoying every second of the attention. With one hand, he comes up to grab my chin and lift my face to his. My mouth welcomes his dripping tongue, and I am eager to swallow each drop. I can feel his passion through his lips, his dedication through his fingers. Once again, I find myself grinding in sync with his thrusts. He senses I am close again and slows his pace. Keeping just enough pressure to maintain my state of bliss without taking me over. He breaks away for a moment and makes his way around to face me directly. He leans closer to my lips before kissing them softly.

"Take some time to soak. I will be back for you soon."

He gives me a look of satisfaction as if he knows I am content in this state of arousal. He walks out and closes the door behind him, and I can hear his footsteps fade away. As much as I wish to play in my wetness and finish what he started, I refuse to rob him of the experience. Melting away in the bath, I fantasize about what is next and my nipples get hard again. A multitude of plans he specially designed to treasure me. After a while and several daydreams later, he comes back in. Shirt off and jeans undone.

Gift Giving:

He approaches me with one arm tucked behind his back. I think nothing of it as he reaches for my hand, assisting me out of the bath. I place my hand on his shoulder and watch his skin glisten as drops of water bead down his sculpted chest. The second I am secure on my feet; I feel his strong arms around me. Quickly and tightly pulling me in. I look at him with admiration and appreciation and both lips begin to tingle. A smirk appears on his face as he bites his bottom lip, looking at me with intentions unknown. He leans in to meet my waiting tongue, and I feel his body pressed against mine. His kisses are so soft, and our breathing begins to match one another as we exchange energies. He suddenly pulls away from me, revealing what he has been hiding all this time. Before my eyes is a brand-new anal plug, designed with me in mind. Gold plated with a perfectly swelled bulb and a name he'd given me engraved into the jeweled base.

"Do you like it?"

His eyes peering into mine, looking for an answer he already knows. I nod with the widest smile.

"I love it."

"Good. You will be wearing it tonight."

He returns his lips to mine, and I feel the satisfying cool touch of metal trailing down the center of my back. Reaching my ass, he teases me by gliding the plug along my curves. With his tongue nearly in my throat, I begin gyrating my hips. Grinding myself into his body while simultaneously dancing to his rhythm. He stops to look me in my eyes and brings the plug up between our lips.

"Stick out your tongue."

I obey as he slides my new treat into my mouth. He lets out a low, grumbly moan as he watches.

"Perfect, baby. Suck it just like that."

His girth begins to swell against my body as I suck and spit all over the gold. He places his fingers under my chin and pulls me closer, never removing his gaze. As he slowly pulls the plug away from my lips, I hold onto him tighter, eagerly awaiting his next move. As the perfect distraction, he grabs me by the cheek with one hand and kisses me deeply as the other gently slides my custom plug inside of me. My breath carries a quiet moan into his mouth with each push deeper. I finally feel some fullness that I have been waiting for. It fits so well, and he is happy with the results. My pussy is aching, throbbing. Begging for his touch, his attention. But I wait patiently, knowing he loves it more when I marinate in my juices and desire. We continue to tangle our tongues while our hands explore each other's body, him occasionally playing with my ass. Barely sliding the plug in and out but just enough for me to feel the sensation. I wonder if he can feel me soaking his pants leg. After a while of receiving this special attention, inside I am screaming for more of him. Right on time, he steps back and holds my hand.

"Come on. I need you now and I am not waiting any longer."

He leads me to the bedroom and stands me at the foot of the bed.

He walks around the bed and lays a blindfold, handcuffs, and a collar on top of the pillows. The perfect set to match my new jewel. The leather is shiny and white with gold chains and locks linking them together. I am amazed by his attention to detail, he knows just what I like the most. His hand reaching out for mine, he assists me onto the bed, guiding me to a sitting position. He looks deep into my eyes. Reading my body language and seeing that I am ready, he picks up the collar and begins to wrap it around my neck. His low and powerful voice in my ear,

"I love that you behave so well for me. My perfect little princess."

I am getting wetter by the second as he takes his time in preparing me to receive all he must give. He secures the lock on my collar with the turn of a key. It is snug and tight around my neck in the most perfect ways. I can feel my body tingling from the inside out. He moves on to bind my hands before reaching for the blindfold. A pause to look upon me once more but instead of lust lingering in his eyes, I saw sincerity.

"I am going to do with you as I please. If at any moment you are uncomfortable, say yellow. If at any moment you wish to stop, say red. I will

not push you past your limits, but you will be punished if you disobey. Do you understand what I am telling you?"

He is so careful with his words and so patient in his questioning. I gaze into him and give him a nod.

"Yes, sir. I understand."

Another soft kiss meets my forehead, and he steps behind me. The blindfold comes down over my face and my pulse quickens as he makes a tight bow, ensuring no peeking. Once I am secured, he makes sure his touch never breaks contact with my skin. I feel his hands glide down my neck, then to my shoulders. His lips show more attention to my chest and stomach as he guides me back, softly laying me down on the bed. He flicks his tongue across my body, missing not a single sweet spot, traveling lower and lower with his hands gripping my thighs tighter and tighter. Finally, his mouth meets the warmth between my legs, and I feel my spirit ascend. I cannot keep the moans of pleasure from escaping my lips as I throw back my head and arch my spine, signaling to him my satisfaction. I cannot see him but knowing that he must be watching me is driving my mind into a frenzy. With my sight obscured, simple bliss begins to feel like an otherworldly journey towards euphoria. His tongue taps and swirls in and around my pussy until I am squirming helplessly in his hands. He makes love to my soul, cherishes my body, and stimulates my mind. I thought I was ready for him, but this pleasure may be too much to endure.

Quality Time:

After taking me to a state of pure ecstasy, he removes the blindfold from my face, and I slowly come out of my fantasies. He is smiling, looking at me as if I make him proud. He has such a way of making me feel safe and adored. He climbs up next to me and kisses my cheek. I reach my hands out, and he unlocks the cuffs. I rub the marks that they left on my skin with adoration. As I pull my hair aside to release my collar, he stops me and reaches for the key. He stands and comes around me, whispering in my ear,

"Good job, baby",

before unlocking me. He removes the collar so tenderly, careful not to cause me any discomfort, and his warm hands sooth my neck where there was the most restriction. His touch just melts me. He senses the weakness in my body and helps me to my feet, leading me to the chaise across the room.

"I'll be right back. Stay here."

I watch as his half-naked body leaves the room. He soon returns with a glass of my favorite wine in one hand and massage oil in the other. As he hands the glass to me, the smell of cashmere and lavender fills the air. He places the oil on the table next to us and sits down, pulling me close. My head rests on his chest, and he takes a drink before setting the glass down and pulling the table closer.

"Lay back. It is still your night. I'm going to take care of you."

I soften my posture and sit back, keeping him in my line of sight. He readies his hands with the oil, and starting with my feet and legs, begins to massage me further into paradise. His hands make their way up, down and around my body, paying special attention to my hips, arms, and thighs. The feeling of him against my bare skin is intoxicating and calming. He puts me in my softest state before his hands separate from me. He softly touches my face and peers into my soul.

"How about we watch something nice, or I read you our favorite book?"

He is always full of surprises. Another one of his ways to make the sensations running through my veins linger even longer. He guides me over to our now made bed as I point out which erotica we will be enjoying for the night. Picking up where we left off, he takes on a tone of luscious sensuality and I unwind under the sheets next to him. His cadence pauses, he looks at me.

"You know, you mean the world to me."

I can see the genuineness in his eyes and the smile that is barely tugging at the corner of his lips. The journey we've embarked on is just the beginning of a much greater adventure, one that promises to please and surprise with each new discovery.

The Weight of Want

MAZOPHILIA

She knew the look.
That slow, unblinking drift of his gaze, dropping from her mouth mid-laugh to settle – deliberately, reverently – on her chest. Not with crude hunger, not with adolescent awe, but with the kind of quiet fixation that made her skin prickle beneath the silk of her blouse.

He'd been watching her like that all evening – over wine, through dessert, in the low hum of conversation – and now, with the door closed behind them and the city's night pressing soft against the windows, his restraint was starting to fray.

"You've been staring," she said, coy and quiet, leaning back against the couch with a deliberate arch of her spine.
"I know." He didn't bother denying it, His voice had a rasp to it now, the kind that suggested

restraint was a game he was tired of playing. "You know what you do to me."

She smiled, slow and knowing. Her fingers found the top button of her blouse and slipped it free. Then another. Then another.
His breath caught – not dramatically, but subtly, like his body was bracing for a pleasure it already knew intimately.

"You want them?" she teased, voice like velvet soaked in sin. She slipped the blouse off her shoulders, varying the soft curve of her breasts, supported by a pale lace bra, barely doing the job.
He dropped to his knees in front of her.
"You know I do."

She unclasped the bra with one flick, letting it fall between them. He exhaled like he'd been punched in the gut. His hands hovered just shy of touching her, reverent, trembling.

"Please," he whispered.
She let him.

His palms cupped them like offerings – warm, full, heavy in his hands. He groaned low in his throat as he lifted and squeezed them, marveling at the give of her flesh, the weight of them filling his hands. His thumbs circled her nipples slowly, watching them stiffen under his touch like they'd been waiting for him all night.

"You love them," she breathed.
"I worship them."

She arched into him as his mouth met her skin – hot, open, insistent. He licked a slow trail from the swell of one breast to the tip, taking her nipple into his mouth with aching reverence. His tongue flicked, suckled, pulled – greedy, but focused. Like he wanted to memorize the taste of her.

Her moan slipped free, soft and sharp.

He moved to the other, lavishing it with equal attention, fingers still kneading and teasing the one he'd left behind. She was throbbing between her thighs now, wet and pulsing, turned on not just by the sensation, but by how utterly captivated he was.

He wasn't thinking about anything else. Not her mouth, not her hips, not even the promise of her slick heat below. Just her breasts – worshiped, devoured, adored like they were his religion.

She gripped his hair, tugging gently.
"What is it about them?" she asked, breathless.
He looked up at her, lips wet, eyes dark.

"They're soft, perfect. Yours. I love how they fit in my hands, how they bounce when you ride me, how you moan when I suck on them -"
He kissed the inner curve, reverent again.
"They drive me fucking insane.

And he showed her.
With his mouth and his tongue, with both hands wrapped around her, he pushed her back into the couch and climbed over her, never once breaking contact with the body part that held him so spellbound. She writhed beneath him, chest rising

and falling with every lick, every groan, every tug of his lips.

When he finally moved lower – kissing down her stomach, between her thighs, tasting the proof of her arousal – she was gasping, boneless, undone.

And when he slid inside her minutes later, deep and slow, her breasts bounced with each thrust – just like he loved. His eyes stayed locked on them, his hands never far, like he couldn't bear to part from his favorite part of her body.

She let him have them – again and again – until they both came undone.
Afterward, still inside her, breath ragged and hearts pounding, he cupped them once more, gently now.

"I could die here," he murmured against her nipple.
She laughed, soft and wicked.
"You just might."

After Party

ADD YOUR ENDING

February 11, 2023

He wants this time to be perfect.

It's their fifth Valentine's Day and for years, he has dreamt of spoiling her with treatment befitting of a queen. She deserves it, after all. A goddess to him, the woman of his dreams. The one who makes his heart pound and his knees weak. She is his muse. His everything. And he will go to any lengths for her satisfaction.

She just wants him.

Year after year, she watches the man she loves learn not only her mind and spirit, but her body as well and all the secrets it keeps. He adorns her with attention and affection. Showers her with whatever she desires. He would give the world if he could, and she knows it. He is her foundation. Her guide and protector. This is going to be her time to return the favor.

"I have something planned for us tonight and I don't want you asking any questions.

The way he gives commands will always send chills through her body. His voice, rich and velvety, is irresistibly alluring. But she knows the best consequences come from disobeying his word.

"Well, what is it?" she asks with the sexy smirk he loves.

With no answer, he turns away and walks to the bedroom. She follows, expecting him to assert his dominance. He turns her around, facing the door so that she cannot know what was next. Those powerful hands of his. One squeezing her ass with the firmest grasp. The other coming around to meet her face.

With a grip of the chin, he tells her,

"Be a good girl and do as you are told."

She forces a slight grin, and her eyes catch a glimpse of what's next to her.

Laying out on the bed for her is a ravishing red gown, matching diamond earrings and the sexiest black lingerie to peek from underneath. Blushing and biting her lip, she looks at him with no words.

He holds her. His strong yet gentle hands wrapping around her waist.

"Get dressed, we leave in thirty minutes."

A soft kiss on the neck before he walks out the door. She is speechless, excited, and anxious for the night to begin. She is already getting wet, wondering what he has planned for her. All she knows is that she will have to focus on containing her excitement. She puts on her gown, the lace lingerie hugging her body tightly, leaving just enough to the imagination. And the night begins.

They arrive at a lavish venue ready to enjoy all the night has to offer. The lights dim, the music slow. He leads her to the bar, his hand sliding down her back to her behind as he reaches for a drink. The heat of his skin and the alcohol rushing through her blook stream has her melting into his touch.

She turns away and begins dancing with her back to his chest, slowly grinding her hips into the fullness of his dress slacks.

His hands roamed over her body, caressing her breasts, running his fingers over her nipples, and finally resting at her waist, pulling her closer. In her ear she hears his hypnotic voice,

"I'm going to finger fuck you so good at dinner. I want to feel you dripping down my hand."

She bites her lip harder and lets out a shy whine. Feeling her fresh, new lingerie become soaked more and more by the second. He leads her to their table, pulling out her chair and placing his hand on her thigh as they sat.

They begin their meal, socializing with guests and talking about their day and work. He keeps his hand on her thigh, his touch burning a hole through her skin. She finds herself writhing in her seat trying to feel the slightest sense of pleasure through her dress. Instead, she feels his grip become tighter, silently telling her to keep still.

He looks at her with eyes that pierce right through her. A warning, a tease. His gaze says it all. Wearing a grin, he asks,

"Will you feed me, please?"

She serves him a taste of the meal before them. As the fork met his lips, his fingers finally met hers. She was almost dripping just like he knew she would be.

They both release a sigh of pleasure at the table. Unbeknownst to all, they are having a party of their own. His fingers play in her wetness as she squirms under the table; barely able to maintain her composure.

With each gyration she makes, his fingers match her rhythm. A secret dance that no one notices. She takes a sip of wine, and he slips two of his fingers inside.

"Oh my god," she musters a whisper and almost tips her glass.

Deflecting a stray glance from the other side of the table. His fingers thrust and curl against her G-spot and his thumb begins to rub her clit as her moans grow louder, but still inaudible over the roar of countless conversations.

He sees the blush rising in her cheeks and how hard her nipples are poking through her dress. As a slow tease, he pulls his fingers out of her and gently taps her pussy. A sign of praise she always adores. He leans over to whisper in her ear,

“I love how wet you get for me. You did such a good job.”

She watches him with lust in her eyes as he sucks her flavor off his fingers and flashes her a devilish grin.

“Mmm, you taste like magic, sugar cane and all I dream of.”

After dinner finished, they make their way to the nearest restroom. She has an idea of what is next, and she can hardly wait. They find the furthest stall and he rushes her inside, pushing her against the wall and kissing her like there was no moment to lose.

His tongue invading her mouth with a passionate hunger. He slides his hands up her thighs, pushing up her dress.

With one hand, he spreads her lips and starts to play with her clit. With the other, she shoves his fingers into her mouth. Finally, she can let out all those cries she has been holding in. Clinging onto both him and the stall door as her legs begin to tremble. She is flowing down to her knees, just as he tells her to get down on them. As she lowers to the ground, her hands dance down his chest as he slightly raises his shirt. Admiring the physique that gives her sex a throbbing heartbeat just by the sight.

She opens her mouth and flicks out her tongue. Savoring the precious precum leaking out of him and swirling it around his tip. She receives him with a hunger that shakes the air between them, sucking and slurping until she could hear the wetness of her mouth.

His low moans turn to deep, rumbling growls that can almost be heard through the restroom door. She starts sucking faster and stronger.

Occasionally, pulling him out for a spit shine before plunging him back into her throat. Her eyes start to water as she feels him getting closer to his peak. Until she pulls away.

"I want to feel you inside of me. But make it quick, we have a party to get back to."

She cannot take the aching between her legs any longer. She feels the pounding in her chest as he helps her to her feet and kisses all the mess she has made.

"I'm going to make you beg for more by the end of the night."

He turns her around, bending her over the toilet. Pulling her panties to the side, revealing her bare, soaking wet pussy.

He cannot help but to stare and admire how pretty her tight little kitten is and he needs a taste. He leans in to get a mouthful of dripping warmth, like the sweetest honey he has ever had the opportunity to savor. As he moans with his mouth against her sweetness, she arches her back and reaches around. Holding his head stable as she twirls and grinds herself deeper into his mouth.

His beard is wet with her juices and his eyes are filled with lust. She is ready for more as he rises and rips away the threads of her lingerie. With a fistful of hair, he pins her against the wall and enters her nice and easy. They both let out a deep breath. Her walls tighten around his dick, gripping and pulling him in further. His tip reaching all the best places inside of her. His fingers dig into her hips, sure to leave bruises that would last the rest of the night.

The sounds of their bliss echoes off the restroom walls and door. Her legs shake and threaten to buckle, her moans and yells growing louder and stronger. Both of them getting close to climax and not caring about if the other guests can hear. She grabs her breast to pinch her nipple between her fingers. Each tug and pull giving her extra sensation to fuel her fire. She lets out a cry of ecstasy,

"Don't stop baby, I'm almost there."

He reaches around to rub her moisture into her clit with small circles. Keeping his fingers directly on her hot spot, ensuring her satisfaction. She is coming so hard, her knees are weak.

Her legs give out and he pulls out just before her orgasm is complete. He turns her around and lifts her up against the wall, her legs now wrapped around her waist. He slides back inside of her as she throws her head back and sighs in relief. His thrusts quicken and go deeper with each stroke, along with their breaths. Her nails rake down his back, causing him to arch in pleasant pain. Suddenly, they both feel their release coming.

"Yes! Just like that. Just like that! Fuck!"

Her canal tightening and pulsating around his cock, squeezing every ounce of pleasure out of him. He feels how much she is leaking, splashing against both of their legs, and cannot hold back any longer.

With a euphoric intensity, he fills her, releasing every drop and painting every in inside of her. He lets out a bellowing grunt as he erupts, struggling to catch his breath. As she feels him throbbing inside, she gives him a final grip before he slides out. Adding a gratifying resistance while subtly begging him not to move any further.

She doesn't want him to leave her. They hold each other in a lingering embrace. Their wet, sweaty bodies intertwined and breathing each other in. His tongue, gliding up her neck, meets hers and dances around her mouth as they melt into one another. Locked in a trance before putting themselves together to return to the party.

With their clothes straightened and appearances made, they return to their assigned seats at the table where their dessert and champagne had been waiting.

"I'm not done with you yet, mister."

She leans over and kisses his neck ever so gently. Giving him a reminder of her insatiable appetite. He looks at her with slight surprise, but knowing the quick restroom session was not enough to fulfill them both. They craved the feeling of the other too much to stop.

She takes a bite of her chocolate truffle, looking him in his eyes. Making sure he knows it is a tease for later. He returns the favor by drinking the last drop of his champagne, licking the rim.

Her mind races with ideas, hoping he will finish what they started. She looks around the room scanning the environment. The dance floor is full of couples dancing slowly, hands exploring all different places.

Her mind drifts to how it would feel if his hands were suddenly all over her body. Sliding his fingers between her folds, making her drip all over again. He leans in and whispers into her ear, his beard tickling her skin, sending a chill down her spine causing a familiar ache forming between her legs.

"Come on, let's go home. I'm ready to devour you."

This night, unlike the others, will not end until he is satisfied that he has shown her every form of love and affection.

Taking her by hand, he helps her to her feet to leave from the table and escorts her to the car waiting outside. They get inside and she sits as close as she can to him, his arm wrapped securely around her.

His fingers begin to trace her inner thigh and all she can think of is what will happen when they are finally in the comforts of their home.

The drive is an agonizing wait. They arrive and quickly walk inside. The second the door closes, he pushes her up against it. With his pressure against her chest, she can't wait for him to touch her, and to get him out of his clothes. He looks at her with desire and whispers,

"I need you."

Her heart begins to beat a little faster, and she responds,

"I need you, too. Now."

He pulls her into his arms, kissing her intently, before his lips travel to her neck, kissing and licking. His hands roam her body freely, gracing her with touches in all the places that make her weak. With a night to remember still lingering in their system, they begin their dance once again.

Foreplay is Core Play

What specific acts during foreplay do you enjoy the most?

How do you like to be touched or held? Where do you want their hands on your body? How long would you like it to last?

Use this space to create tips & tricks that a partner can learn from or to find new ways to get you fired up.

A breath.
Then another – shaky, shallow.
Fingertips slide low.

A soft moan, barely there.
Caught between lips.
Held like a secret.

Clothes peel away.
A gasp, sharp and sudden.
Skin, warm and waiting.

The sound – wet, rhythmic.
A hum behind teeth.
A whimper chased by a sigh.

Back arches.
Fingers dig in.
The moan deepens.

No words.
Just breath and want.

A kiss, dragged slow.

A cry – bitten back.
Body trembling.

A pause.
Then pressure.
Then... that moan.

The kind that rises.
The kind you can feel.
In your chest. In your sex.

Uncontrolled.
Unapologetic.
A surrender in sound.

Stillness.
Sweat.
A quiet whimper, fading.

No names.
No promises.
Only moans.

Reminisce

Describe your most intense intimate experience. Describe every sound, smell, taste, and sensation. What made it unforgettable? Would you do it again – or differently?

A Scene to Be Seen

AUTAGONISTOPHILIA

Anniversary nights always brought something a little different. But this year, it was the view – not the wine, not the setting – that made her legs tremble.

The city stretched below them, glittering and unaware – or so they thought. On the high-rise balcony, under nothing but the moonlight and his roaming hands, she pressed against the railing, hips bare, breath catching in sync with the pulse of traffic far below.

She loved being on display, even in imagined secrecy. But this time, it wasn't imagined.

Across the way, lights flickered on in a window directly opposite. A man and woman, tangled in shadows, stared back with equal hunger. Watching. Moving. Matching. They weren't ashamed – they were emboldened.

The distance dissolved. Two couples, each fueled by the thrill of being seen, caught in a mirrored performance where climax became currency, and the city became an unknowing voyeur.

She didn't flinch. If anything, her back arched harder into his hands as she looked across at the open window. Her fingers slid up the railing, bracing herself as he knelt behind her, parting her thighs with a low groan.

"Look," she whispered, eyes trained on the couple across the gap. "They're watching."

"I know," he said, the scrape of his voice teasing down her spine. "They like what they see."

She felt the warmth of his mouth between her thighs before she could answer, the slow drag of his tongue over her already aching center. She moaned, loudly, intentionally – half for him, half for the strangers across the way. Her knees buckled, and he steadied her, spreading her wider.

On the other side, the woman sat on the edge of a windowsill, legs open, her partner kneeling just like him. Their eyes locked for a long, loaded moment.

Fuck, she mouthed silently.
And fuck, they did.

His mouth didn't let up, lips slick and greedy, tongue curling inside her with the skill of a man who loved to show off. Her head fell back, chest heaving, nipples hard in the night air. She caught movement from the other side – the other woman now bent forward, hands pressed to the glass, her man entering her from behind.

Their rhythm synced. Her moans echoed hers. Their pleasure – shared, mirrored, multiplied.

"You're dripping," he murmured as he stood, his fingers stroking through the wetness he'd coaxed from her. "They can see how ready you are."

"I want them to see everything."

He didn't hesitate. He turned her to face the window, one hand gripping her throat, the other guiding himself between her legs. The first thrust knocked the breath out of her lungs. Deep, hard, possessive.

"Let them watch you fall apart."

For Your Eyes Only

What's a fantasy you've never told anyone – because it felt too taboo, too wild, too much? Describe it like it's about to happen tonight. Who's involved? Where are you? What are you doing first?

2's Company, 3's A Crowd, 5's An Unforgettable Night

I first introduced my husband, Aaron, to my best friend Brooke a few years ago when we ran into her at our coffee shop. I had known her ever since middle school and we frequently texted each other on birthdays and holidays but had yet been able to make time for each other.

Brooke was a wildcard and a pure hedonist. The kind of friend that you never really knew where they were or what they were doing, but you always knew it was probably something exciting. She was about 5'3" with big, brown eyes, almost doe-like. With long, curly hair and a shape that would make anyone stop and stare. Including me, but I'd never tell her that secret. How does one tell their best friend that the mere sight of them gets you going. I didn't want to push that boundary.

When we ran into her at the shop that day, I was ecstatic to be seeing her again. We talked about everything under the sun – from how much we missed one another to the last movie we saw. She told us about her husband who she'd met two years prior and how they discovered their shared desire to explore exhibitionism. This didn't surprise me because Brooke always loved being seen in her best moments. What surprised me was her proposal.

She invited Aaron and me to double date her and her husband, Scott. "He's a blast," she mentioned, "I met him at a friend's bachelorette party when I was giving lap dances, you know me." Her smile big and bright as she recalls the night. "And so, he sat in the chair, I did a little dance, and before we knew it, we were in a closet tearing each other's clothes off before he bent me over and gave me the best five-minute fuck of my life."
We laughed because this was just her style, indulging in pleasure whenever the opportunity presented itself. From all she told us, Scott seemed like a good match for her and a good guy overall, so we agreed to meet them at a new restaurant in town.

We all arrived around the same time to be seated at our table. Brooke and Scott both looked amazing. She was wearing the most gorgeous, sparkly, black gown I had ever seen her in, and Scott was more appealing than I had imagined. He was tall with sandy blonde hair and hazel eyes, a slim fit physique, and a voice like my husbands. Low and raspy with a hint of mystery, drawing you in like a captivating melody.

"Hey, nice to meet you both. I'm Scott, Brooke's husband."

I couldn't peel my eyes away from this ravishing couple standing in front of me while handshakes and hugs were being exchanged.

After getting settled and looking over the menu, our drinks were brought to the table and conversation started to flow. We laughed at jokes, talked about our jobs, and discussed the things we did in our spare time.

Aaron was having the most fun and I could tell. He was laughing so hard, throwing back shots, and telling his most embarrassing stories. It was like he was on a high from our company, like he was drunk on them. I can't pretend as if I wasn't feeling the same. Their energy was exhilarating, and we fed off it.

The more their fingers danced with each other, the more I'd brush my leg against Aaron's. Every time they'd kiss, I'd imagine it was Aaron's lips on my neck. Watching them made me want to devour my husband right there at the table. By the time our meals arrived, we were all about two drinks in and reveling in each other's company and conversation.

It was Brooke and I who noticed our server. A petite red headed woman with emerald, green eyes, and a model-like figure. She was astonishing, an appealing image to match her hospitable manner and politeness. She said her name was Irina and we had been watching her most of the night. Brooke knew of my interest in women and loved to play matchmaker for the fun of it. Never thinking she would be taken seriously. But tonight was a little different. She and Scott made me want to try new things and take risks.

While the guys were discussing miniscule matters, she leaned over the table and whispered, "I dare you to invite her home with us."

Us? She couldn't have been implying what I thought she was. Right when I was fixing my lips to ask for clarification, I saw a shift in her eyes. A look that went from platonically friendly to seductive and persuasive.

She looked at Scott, then reassuringly back at me. It was a look that told me, she was serious. My stomach dropped, my heartbeat quickened, and my throat felt dry. I wasn't expecting this, but the thrill of the thought was overwhelming. I nudged Aaron, secretly telling him I needed to talk. Once away from the table, I told him about what I believed was being proposed.

"I think Brooke wants us to go home with them. She told me to invite our server!"

His jaw dropped and he looked shocked. I was afraid he'd march back over to the table and cause a scene objecting to the idea. Instead, he just chuckled and smiled.

"Well honey, it's your call. This is your night."

I couldn't believe it. My husband had just given me the okay to have sex with my best friend and her husband. And to make things more exciting, he told me there were no limits to the pleasure I wanted to receive. I was so horny that the wetness between my legs was starting to leak through my panties. This was the perfect opportunity to indulge in a fantasy, especially after how well the evening was going.

We sauntered back to our table and sat down. Brooke and Scott were watching us return as if matters had been discussed in our absence. "So...", Scott was looking at me, "...about that dare Brooke had for you."
I was nervous and blushing. I had never approached a woman before let alone invite one home for group sex with two random couples. But like my husband said, this was my night, and everyone was dedicating themselves to my pleasure. When our server returned to check on us, that's when I popped the question.

"Is everything going smoothly here? May I offer anyone anything else at the moment?"
Her smile was both warm and welcoming.
"Actually, Irina, we would love it if you were free enough to join us after dinner."

Her face reddened immediately as she flashed a giddy grin.

"Um, well may I ask who's asking?"

"Goodness, my apologies. My name is Brianne. This is my husband Aaron, my best friend Brooke, and her husband Scott. Tonight, we're celebrating...friendship."

Brooke and I looked at each other and smiled.

"Nice to officially meet you all. I won't finish my shift until around twelve but if you all don't mind waiting, I'd love to join."

I turned to the group and was met with three assuring looks.

"Perfect, we'll have drinks after dinner and wait for you."

She walked away smiling as she greeted another table. My husband glanced at me and licked his lips as if he could already taste both her and I simultaneously. I could barely contain my excitement as I imagined having all these bodies clinging onto mine. It was going to be the perfect end to a perfect night.

After dinner, we ordered drinks and dessert and waited for our new friend to arrive. We chatted a bit more, flirted with one another, and took pictures together. I was having a blast.

Irina came back over and told us she was done with her shift, so we decided to head to a local bar to get to know one another a little more before diving into existential bliss. I couldn't tell if she knew of our plans or if she was just a willing and free spirit. Either way, we were all enjoying her energy.

The conversation continued.

"So, Irina," my inhibitions were nearly non-existent by this point, so I was much more willing to divulge in the topic at hand.

"Where are you from?"

"Well, jag är frän Sverige."

Her native tongue was mesmerizing even though I had no clue what she had just told us. She chuckled and restated,

"I'm from Sweden. I moved here when I was twelve years old."

My mind started racing a million miles per second. I always had a thing for European women and the way they carried themselves. So sophisticated and graceful. She was a vision, and her accent was a melody that would send everyone into a spiral. She was so pretty, and I couldn't wait to have her alone with us.

As the night went on, I could sense all the changes in the air as everyone's mood changed from having good ole' fun to being noticeably hot and bothered within minutes. Granted, after three rounds of shots, who wouldn't be at least a little bit turned on being surrounded by such enticing individuals.

We initially broke the ice by playing games like Truth or Dare and Would You Rather, except we tried the explicit versions of course. I remember Brooke had asked me,
"Would you rather, moan in my mouth while I finger you or play with yourself watching me and my husband tongue fuck each other's mouths?" Or when Scott not so subtly dared my husband to rub his dick under the table.

In a common setting, these words would be the least likely to leave my lips, but this group made me comfortable beyond measure, and I was glad to have this moment with them.

After a few more exchanges of "touch me here" and "my mouth here or your mouth there", I could tell that everyone was about ready to take things somewhere more private. I hated to cut the fun short, but I knew better things awaited at home. It was also time to see whether Irina was going to make or break our night.

The guys left the table for a final restroom break, so I took advantage of the moment to ask our guest to continue her night with us.

"Hey, Irina," she looked at me with those eyes I could get lost in forever, "I think I speak for everyone when I say, you have been an amazing time tonight and we're not sure we want it to end just yet."

Flashing a grin, she responds,

"I'm really enjoying you all as well. I rarely meet people as attractive and friendly as everyone here.

But I know why you asked me to join you here. Name the next destination, I'll be there."

She took a sip of her drink as I struggled to control my excitement. As the gentlemen returned to the table, Brooke flashed them a sly wink, letting them know that tonight was in fact going as planned. We closed our tab and began walking to our cars. Irina decided to meet us at Brooke and Scott's house. The time had finally come to live out my innermost fantasies.

Once inside the home, the air felt hot. No one had said a word, but we could all feel it. The energy was intense, the air was thick, and everyone was on fire. There was palpable electricity in the room, and I wanted it to shock me.

"Everyone, welcome inside. Please, make yourselves comfortable. I'll grab us some wine."

Brooke was always an amazing host, and this time was no different. In fact, it was best for us all that she executed this role with her usual grace. Making our way to the living room, I took a seat on the sofa next to Irina, being sure to leave room for Brooke. Scott sat in a chair near the fireplace across from us ladies and my husband adjacent to him.

Brooke returned swiftly with a bottle of Russian River Valley Pinot Noir. The perfect pairing for our night.

Once glasses were poured, everyone made attempts to ignore the sexual tension in the air and maintain lively conversation. It wasn't until Brooke made the first move that those tensions were finally broken.

"You know, I just can't take this anymore." She sat her glass down on the table and ever so softly grabbed Irina by the cheek. With no hesitation, she went in for a kiss. Barely waiting before sliding her tongue inside Irina's mouth. For a second, everyone simply watched these two beautiful women dance their tongues around each other's. But I wasn't waiting long before having fun as well.

I brushed back Irina's hair and began kissing and sucking her neck. Her moans told me all I needed to know, *keep going*. She turned around slightly to better align herself with my lips. The tip of her tongue traced my mouth as I breathed her in. Needing all she had to give; I gently kissed her mouth and pulled at her bottom lip with my teeth. Irina moaned, and I could hear a similar noise coming from across the room.

Opening my eyes, I saw Scott had slid his hand in his pants and was gripping his dick. I understood now why Brooke loved every inch of him. All inches of him, as I could see through his pants that he was endowed much like my husband. Aaron, still playing coy, struggled to remain still in his seat. Repeatedly adjusting himself as his pants grew tighter. As the guys enjoyed the show, so did Irina, as she was the star.

She tasted Brooke and I in intervals. When Brooke had her attention, I would glide my tongue down Irina's back, sending her chills that would make her body twist and jerk in my hands. When her lips returned to mine, Brooke would grip and squeeze Irina's breasts, gently twisting her nipples between her fingers. Our sighs of pleasure were so harmonious, I couldn't tell them apart.

Without losing my focus, I noticed Scott get up from his seat and make his way over to my husband. I heard him whisper in Aaron's ear, "Why don't we join them?"
and all I could think of was how much I welcomed the idea.
He got Aaron out of his seat and they both walked over to the sofa.

Scott started caressing Brooke's neck and chest as if he was inside her skin. She was all over Irina, stretching her hands over to my thighs while my husband massaged my shoulders.
I felt Aaron's hand reaching around the front of my throat and squeezing firmly. He tilted my chin up towards him, told me to open my mouth, and pursed his lips. I closed my eyes awaiting my treat and felt his wet saliva drip into my mouth.
The taste of him made me instantly wetter, I couldn't keep my fingers from softly stroking my throbbing pussy through my panties. I return my attention to the women beside me.

Irina was licking Brooke's breasts, gently tugging on her nipples with her teeth, while Brooke's tongue was exploring her husband's mouth. As she kissed Scott, she made a point to look at me, her way of saying, don't be shy, do something. So, I did.

I crouched down on the floor in front of her and used the remaining saliva my husband left in my mouth to moisten her inner thigh.
I kissed and nibbled my way up until I felt her squirming. Gyrating her hips every which way to feel something deeper than my lips could provide. I could feel the warmth radiating from between her legs onto my face. The smell of her was both enticing and intoxicating, worsening the wait to savor her flavor.

I took the tip of my tongue and softly traced my initials just near the lining of her silky, lace lingerie. She let out a whimper of pleasure as she ran her fingers through my hair and down the back of my neck. She was struggling to speak but her body was begging for more.

My fingers found their way inside her panties, slowly and gently gliding up and down her labia, and I immediately felt her wetness. She was gushing.
I used my middle and ring fingers to separate her inner and outer lips and stimulated her clitoris directly. And as her head was thrown back in bliss, kissing her husband with Irina enjoying mine, I realized that at this point, everyone had completely invested themselves in the festivities.

I looked up from Brooke and saw Scott and Aaron both had pulled out their cocks. Slowly stroking themselves watching us women indulge in each other's essence.
My husband had a firm grip on his shaft as if he was trying to restrain his excitement. I could see precum forming at the head and it took everything in me not to get up and lick it clean. I didn't want to be selfish.

Irina was still enjoying Brooke before I gently grabbed her by the arm.
"Here, come taste."

I held her chin as she flicked out her tongue and lapped up every drop that was oozing out of him.
"No no, don't swallow just yet."
I couldn't miss the chance to taste the satisfactory mix that was them. I swirled my tongue around the inside of her mouth, nearly reaching the back of her throat. She matched my energy by dropping her hand to my crotch and playing with my clit through my thong. I could feel the heat coming off me in waves.
With the other hand, she took her thumb and slowly circled it around the head of Aaron's dick, then wiped the juices off and put it in my mouth.

Her mouth was watering, and she licked the drool clean from the corner of her lips. Brooke, feeling as if she was missing out on some fun, got up and came around to our side of the sofa. Her husband followed suit and positioned himself behind Aaron.
As my husband's hands caressed my body and Irina's mouth made love to mine, Brooke positioned herself between my thighs and separated them with the back of her hands.

With one swift motion after licking her pretty, plump lips, she went in to devour me.

I cried out with passion. I could feel every lap of her tongue against all my sweet spots. The way she spit on my clit and slurped it back into her mouth would make my body quiver. Not to mention the pleasure I was receiving from my husband and someone who was once just our hospitable server.

While the three were all over me, Scott reached around Aaron and gently held his thick, pulsing dick. My husband hesitated, being that he'd never been intimate with another man before. But one look at me gave him the power he needed to submit himself to a new experience.
In some way, Scott knew just how to use his wrists to please my husband. Aaron was reveling in having this new man slide his hands up, down and around his shaft and tip.

Scott's hard cock pressed against Aaron's ass. My husband, wanting to be generous, would occasionally reach behind and grab Scott, jerking him simultaneously. Their breathing picked up as did their pace.

Brooke and Irina had their mouths on me while their hands were exploring each other. Irina would alternate between kissing me and stroking my husband. Brooke would switch between tongue fucking my pussy and using that same tongue to swap fluids with Irina. Scott would sometimes use his precum to lube up Aaron. And this went on for a short while before things changed.

We could all tell the energy was rising as the room got warmer and the sounds got louder. I couldn't contain myself any longer. The girls were devouring me, and I could feel myself about to climax. Irina pulled away as if she could read my mind. She seductively looked at me, then at Aaron and said in her enchanting accent,

"Get in my mouth."

I moaned and pushed Brooke's mouth onto me harder as I watched my husband obey Irina's commands.

His strong dick entered her mouth, and he released a deep sigh as he reached the back of her throat. She kept a steady tempo as she sucked him off. Pulling him out of her mouth, circling her tongue around his tip before plunging him back deep inside. Her mouth was dripping saliva and was producing the most beautiful wet noises. I was coming in Brooke's mouth listening to the sucking, slurping, and gagging happening right beside me.

Scott positioned himself behind his wife and finally entered her from behind. She let out a loud and long sigh as he slowly stretched her walls. Everyone had found their starting position. After a while of sucking and stroking, I decided it was time to further our adventures in the bedroom.

The men stood behind their respective women, with Irina in the middle, as we all faced each other. Scott and Aaron rubbing their dicks against our asses, starting with their tips right at our dripping entrances to gather some wetness and glide their way up.

We were all getting a taste of the different bodies in the room. Irina and Brooke were taking turns making out with each other while rubbing their nipples together. They were so into each other that they could barely focus on the men.
My husband was behind me, holding his cock against my pussy, teasing me with the thought of entry. Scott had his tip in Brooke, shallowly rocking his hips back and forth, edging her before going back deep inside.

We hardly made it to the California king-sized bed before more openings were filled. Scott couldn't pull himself out of his wife as he lay on top of her, kissing her like no one else was in the room. I placed myself next to them, lying on my back, and asked Irina to return her tongue to my wet, hot waiting lips. It was like I came the moment I felt her tongue on me. I could feel my sweet secretions running down the crack of my ass.
Aaron came around behind her, tracing her body with his fingers before slowly sliding himself inside her tight walls. She gasped, pleasantly surprised by his length and girth. But she didn't

stop licking. Each stroke inside of her made her mouth jerk against my pussy. Her pleasure was also mine.

I reached over and grabbed Scott's ass, helping him thrust in and out of my best friend who was in paradise. Brooke, appreciating my attentiveness to her pleasure, reached out and started rubbing my nipple. Sliding it between her fingers and around her palm, using her juices as a glide.
I felt the sensation in my core. It was an incredible feeling to be in such a euphoric environment.

Scott switched his position, and Brooke was now straddling him. He slid his hand behind my back and pulled me over. Arranging me to have my ass onto his face and before he used his tongue to lap up every bit of my pussy that was dripping from Irena.
I could feel his breath on me as he struggled to breathe while his wife was riding him.

Irina found a position making out with Brooke while their tongues alternated between one another's. Aaron found himself between them. One would use their mouth to swallow him whole while the other's tongue made figure eights around his balls.

I could tell he loved the attention he was getting as his eyes rolled to the back of his head.

Scott was still licking me, but his fingers were exploring my asshole. I moaned with approval, and he slid his index finger inside. I gripped his head with my thighs and started fucking his face, rubbing my pussy all over his beard. By this time, Brooke and Irina had swapped places. Irina, now riding Scott into oblivion, reached for me, and was playing with my breasts while Brooke watched. My husband laid beside me and Scott while Brooke slid down onto him, Aaron's hands grabbing her thighs and massaging her clit with his thumbs.

Both ladies were having the time of their lives giving their best cowgirl impressions. I leaned over to meet my husband's lips, perched and waiting for me. Our tongues mixed and mingled as everyone was simultaneously giving and receiving pleasure.

Irina reached for Brooke's soft, supple ass and teased her hole with the pad of her fingertip. Brooke glanced over with a begging look in her eye.

Irina's finger slipped inside her behind and Brooke used her hips to rock herself back and forth between my husband's dick and our new friend's finger.

While the couples were fucking, we were all making out with one another.

Sometimes simultaneously, sometimes in shifts. Our moans and whimpers could probably be heard through the walls, and it only made us louder. I was ready to come, and I knew I couldn't be the only one. Our movements became frantic and erratic. Everyone was reaching the edge.

Scott now had Irina bent over in doggy style, spanking her while her tongue was in Brooke. The guys were switching back and forth between our three holes and their hands were all over us. We were one big, hot, sticky mess. Our bodies coated in sweat, cum, and saliva.

Scott started stroking Irina harder and faster. The sound of his hips colliding with her ass and his balls smacking against her wet pussy was the icing on the cake. Aaron, fucking me and watching, started to release his low, rumbly growls, a specific sound that let me know he was seconds from exploding. And I was right there with him, ready to erupt. As the group grew louder, paces quickened, and breaths turned short and shallow.

"Fuck!" "Oh, my God." "Please, don't stop." "Yes, right there!" "Almost baby, almost."

Everyone was eagerly expressing their desire to climax, and it was almost time. After a few more moments of this bliss, I could see Scott and Aaron begin to tense up. Irina and Brooke were close. I knew the perfect way to end this night.

I reached around to grab my husband's ass with both hands, driving his hips deeper into me with each thrust as my legs wrapped around his waist. I could feel the heat coming off him. The sweat on his chest pressed against mine and his lips grazed my neck. I lost control every time he slid inside of me, and I had to release.

"Yes, baby please. Make me come."
He fucked me harder, staring at Brooke's tits as they bounced in rhythm with Scott's strokes through Irina. Brooke was arriving as well, holding Irina's head in place, keeping her tongue on her favorite side of her clit. She cried out in ecstasy,
"Oh, my God, Irina. I'm going to come in your mouth. Are you ready, honey?"
Irina hummed in acceptance as she continued lapping up Brooke's sweet dew.

After more licking and stroking, the ladies were coming simultaneously and the gentlemen followed, filling whichever opening they were currently inside. Each one of us let out a cry of satisfaction as our bodies tightened and convulsed.
Brooke threw back her head and reached out for my hand as I clung onto my husband, feeling his cum running down my walls. She held onto me as Irina dug her nails into her hips, Scott emptying his self deep inside of Irina's tight, gushing cunt.

Our harmonious noises filled the room along with the essence of pure ecstasy. None of us wanted to move an inch as our bodies seemed laced together by lust. Breaths were labored and we laid in our final positions as it became a game of 'whoever speaks first, loses'. But after tonight, it was clear that there were no losers among us. Only victors.

After a while, we managed to catch our breath and clean ourselves up. Once everyone had settled, we sat on the floor talking and laughing again, enjoying each other.
After a while, Irina announced that she would be heading home, and we bid her farewell. I made sure to properly see her out.

"Irina, thank you for being such a special part of our night. We literally couldn't have done this without you, and you made me realize why I wouldn't want to."
She smiled and gently kissed my cheek. "Brianne, you've made me realize why I should get out more often. Thank you for inviting me over, it was an extreme pleasure meeting everyone. And please,

feel free to reach out next time an adventure is needed. You know where to find me."

And with a wink, she walked away to her car, slowly fading into the dark night.

I walked back inside and took a long look at the group sitting in front of me, elated over the memories just created. I didn't know where things would go from here, but I knew no matter what, this was going to be a night to remember for years to come.

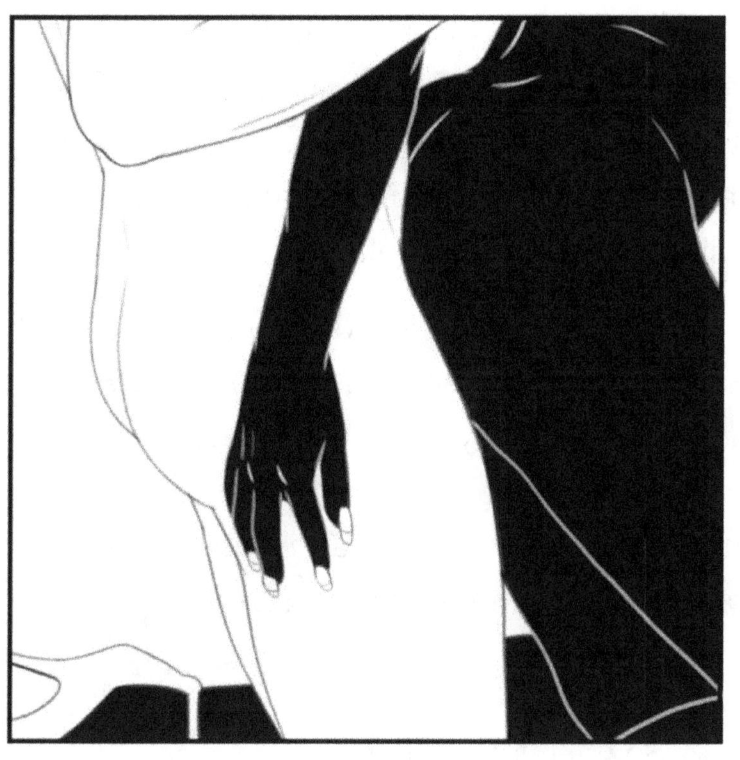

To My Russian Roulette:

I didn't know why you wanted me.

Not really.

You were older – much older – with that sharp accent and steady gaze that made me feel both exposed and elevated. You carried yourself like a man who'd seen things. Had things. Taken things. And I… I was still learning what it meant to be desired for more than softness or youth.

But when you looked at me, it wasn't with hunger alone. It was with intention. You watched me like you already knew what I sounded like when I moaned. Like you'd already decided what kind of lover I would be – and were simply waiting for the moment to confirm it.

So, I let you have me.

I told myself it might just be lust. That maybe I was just young, pretty, convenient. But I let you into my room – and then my body – anyway.

It felt like a gamble. Like slipping a bullet into the chamber and spinning the barrel. But if I was going to risk something, it might as well be for the way you made me feel seen.

You touched me like a man with no rush. No agenda. No need to prove. Your hands didn't grope – they listened. Brushed softly over my skin like you were translating a language only you could hear. Your lips never stopped moving. Not talking – kissing. My neck, my shoulders, my breasts. My stomach. The space between my thighs. Over and over. Again, and again. Like you were kissing away every man who came before you and reminding me that this was new. Different. Yours.

And when you sank between my legs, I stopped asking questions.

You didn't devour me like a man starving. You tasted me like I was your favorite dish – one you'd missed for far too long and needed to savor slowly. Thoroughly.

You licked me like you knew I'd never be the same again. And I haven't been.

I don't remember what music was playing. I don't remember what we said. But I remember the softness of your mouth, the warmth of your breath, the way you pulled me to the edge again and again until I was shaking – crying out in a voice I didn't recognize as my own.

And still, you kissed me. Even when you slid inside me, finally, gently, you didn't rush. You didn't chase. You simply held me, barely moving, letting the weight of your presence – and your care – fuck me in a way that no thrust ever could.

You made me feel...worthy. Not just wanted.

Worthy of time.

Of softness.

Of being touched like I wasn't just beautiful, but unforgettable.

I didn't know why you wanted me.

I still don't.

But I'd let you kiss me like that again, even if it was only ever meant to happen once.

I took the risk.

And you were worth the bullet.

Perfect Pairings

There's a time and a mood for every pour, everybody, every craving.

Pinot Noir is the slow seduction – gentle yet haunting. He kisses like silk and lingers like a secret. His touch is delicate, never rushed, but it unravels you all the same. Beneath that soft-spoken charm lies a surprising depth – earthy, moody, with just enough edge to make your thighs tense when he speaks low in your ear. He doesn't demand; he invites. And when you finally give in, it's like slipping into velvet: warm, familiar, and deeply intoxicating.

Cabernet Sauvignon is bold, unapologetic – the kind of man who grips your hips like hoe owns them and tells you to look him in the eyes when you come. He's full-bodied and rich, layered with spice and dominance, a lover of control and intensity. His kisses taste like crushed berries and power, and when he touches you, it's with purpose. No hesitation. No fluff. Just the raw, primal rhythm of a man who knows exactly what he wants – and exactly how to make your knees forget how to stand.

Malbec is your midnight craving. Smoldering. Complex. He carries the heat of late summer and the promise of things unspoken. There's a darkness to him, not cruel but carnal – a deep plum sweetness laced with peppery fire. He fucks like he means it – hands rough, mouth hungry, voice a low growl as he drags you to the edge and keeps you there, trembling. With Malbec, you don't make love – you burn.

Riesling is the unexpected flirt – sweet on the tongue but with a surprising bite. Playful, cheeky, and always a little too curious, he teases you with soft lips and featherlight fingers until you're aching for more. He'll have you laughing in his lap before sliding two fingers beneath your panties mid-sentence. He tastes of nectar and sunshine but make no mistake – he knows what he's doing.

You think you're leading the dance, but he's already got your skirt hitched and your breath caught.

Sauvignon Blanc is crisp, electric – the lover who tastes like citrus and sea salt, who fucks you on the kitchen counter with the fridge still open. He's vibrant and alive, sparking nerve endings you didn't know you had. Light but insistent, his rhythm quickens with your breath, each thrust like a sip of something sharp and clean that jolts you fully awake. His love is a high – fast, wild, and fleeting – but god, does it leave a mark.

Chardonnay is polished, poised – a man who knows luxury and expects pleasure to come as elegantly as his cufflinks. He speaks in a slow drawl, touches you with practiced grace, and takes his time like foreplay is a fine art. But beneath that sophistication is a heat you don't see coming – a creamy, buttery decadence that blooms on the tongue and blooms even more between your legs when he finally slides inside. With Chardonnay, restraint is the kink, and indulgence is the reward.

Port Wine is the afterglow. The slow exhale. Older, wiser, thick with experience. He doesn't rush. He waits – watches – then devours. His kisses are syrupy, decadent, meant to be savored. He wants you spent, soft, sated in candlelight, and he'll take his time getting you there. With fingers like velvet and a tongue that knows stories, he makes pleasure feel eternal. When you're wrapped in him, drunk and dripping, the world outside simply doesn't exist.

Each lover a vintage, every craving a perfect pour.
I don't choose favorites – I savor them all.

The zipper stopped halfway.

They caught the reflection behind them –

Leaning, watching, breath held.

Didn't turn.

Just rolled their hips and smiled in the mirror.

They pushed the jeans down slow, letting the fabric cling.

Every inch of skin revealed felt deliberate.

Bare thighs, bare ass, a soft sigh escaping.

They stepped out like they knew they were being filmed.

The shirt came next – lifted slow, dragged over their chest.

Nipples peaked in the cool air, exposed to the golden light.

They arched, stretched, letting it fall to the floor.

Still, they didn't speak.

One hand slid over their own breast, teasing, pinching lightly.

The other traced below the navel, slipping beneath soft fabric.

Fingers found heat.

They moaned – just enough for it to carry.

The watcher still hadn't moved.

Didn't have to.

Their silence screamed.

Eyes locked, lips parted, aching to touch.

"You like watching me touch myself?"

They didn't wait for an answer.

Pulled the panties to the side.

Dipped two fingers into wet heat.

The mirror gave them everything – flushed cheeks, heavy-lidded eyes, parted lips.

They fucked themselves slow, keeping the pace unhurried.

A show. A warning.

This was theirs to control.

And behind them, still frozen, the watcher trembled.

Lust in Letters

Write a letter to a past lover – or future one. Tell them exactly what you'd do to them if you had one night with no consequences. Leave nothing out.

Part Two

Dark Flame

After the Scene

After you've been dominated and used, what do you need? What emotions flood your body after the high? How do you want to be held… or not at all?

My Man's Fantasy
MMF

He told me a week in advance what he wanted. "I've got someone. He'll be here on Friday night. I want you ready."

That was all. No softness. No long conversation. Just instructions. And I followed them.

When Friday came, I wore what he left out for me – red lingerie, sheer stockings, heels. He didn't say a word when I walked into the living room. Just stared, slow and cold, eyes trailing over every inch like he was inspecting a piece of work he owned. Which he did.

He pointed to the floor. "On your knees."
I obeyed.

We waited in silence, the only sound being the occasional clink of ice in his glass. When the door finally opened, he didn't move. Didn't even turn his head.

"Lock it," he said. "Then take off your clothes."
The man obeyed.

He was bigger than I expected. Muscled, tattooed, heavy in his movements. I kept my eyes on the floor until my man snapped his fingers once.

"Look at him."
I did.
He was hard already.
"Touch her," my man said. "But don't fucker her until I say so."

The stranger came forward. His hands were rough, fingers calloused. He grabbed my chin, tilted my head back, and dragged his thumb across my lips. I opened for him without being told. He pushed in slowly, making me taste the salt of his skin.

He stood me up and bent me over the edge of the couch, one hand gripping my throat as the other slid down between my thighs. I was soaked – my body betraying just how ready I was for this. He pushed my panties aside, teasing the slick folds, spreading me open like he was studying every detail.

Behind us, I heard my man's voice – steady, calm.
"Let her beg."

The stranger chuckled, deep and quiet, and pulled his fingers out of me. I whimpered. He smacked my ass – once, twice – then rubbed the sting with his palm.

"Beg for it."
I did.

He teased me with the head of his cock, sliding against my slit, tapping against my entrance, pushing just enough to make me twitch and gasp.

Then my man spoke again. "Fuck her."
He drove into me hard.

No warning. No easing in. Just full, raw force. I cried out, my face pressed into the cushions, ass up, his body slamming against mine with every thrust. My man stayed seated, watching, stroking himself lazily.

"Open her up," he told him. "Let me see everything."

The stranger reached around and spread me wider. My man stood, moved behind us, watching up close, hands on my lower back. Then he leaned in.

"Now take her mouth."

This muscled man pulled out of my cunt, dragged me by the hair until I was on my knees again. He shoved his cock past my lips, and I opened wide, letting him fuck my throat while my man moved behind me.

He pushed in fast, already hard, already impatient.

The rhythm was brutal – his cock pounding into my pussy while the other man used my mouth like it was his right. I gagged, tears pricking the corners of my eyes, but I didn't stop. Couldn't. I was their toy, their plaything, their shared possession.

They used me like they'd rehearsed it.
And I loved it.

When I started to tremble, my man pulled out and slapped my ass.
"Not yet."
I whimpered, desperate for release.

They flipped me, legs spread wide, two cocks rubbing against my soaked entrance. One inside, one in my mouth, then switching –

over and over until I was crying from the stretch and the intensity. It wasn't romance. It wasn't affection. It was consumption.

My orgasm hit hard – body shaking, back arching, breath gone. They didn't stop. They fucked me through it, chasing their own release, using every inch of me until they were finished.

The room fell quiet – thick with sweat, hear, and the aftershock of indulgence.

My man pulled away first. He didn't say anything, just stood, slid on his briefs, and walked to the window. The other man followed, heading toward the bathroom without a glance.

I stayed where I was – legs parted, body still pulsing, heart hammering in my throat. Not broken. Not ruined. Just...used to completion.

When the door closed behind the other man, my partner turned and looked at me.
Not with softness. Not with guilt.
With pride.

"You did well," he said. "Better than I imagined."
I met his gaze, unsmiling, still breathless.
"Is that it?" I asked.

He stepped closer, crouched down, and ran two fingers down the side of my neck, tracing the heat of my skin.
"For now."

Then he stood again, lit a cigarette, and walked out – leaving me there in the quiet, every nerve still burning, every part of me humming with the knowledge that the game had only just begun.

To My Forbidden Affair:

You always had a smell I couldn't shake. It was raw, almost feral. And intoxicating, like your essence was made to appease my senses. It clung to you like heat after a storm and emanated in every room you entered. I breathed it in like it belonged to me, and maybe, in some twisted way, it did for a while.

We never had a bond. No innocent memories to cloud what we became. You weren't my friend. You weren't anything, really. Just familiar enough to know better, and distant enough to do it anyway.

It didn't start with conversation. It wasn't born from laughter or shared stories. It was a look – longer than it should've been. Then another. And another. Until the silence between us grew heavy and thick with understanding.

You wanted me.

And I?

I didn't flinch.

We crossed that line without hesitation. No awkwardness, no guilt – just heat. The kind that coils low and takes over. I remember the first time like a secret pressed against my spine – rough hands, muffled breath, the unmistakable sound of knowing this was wrong and doing it anyway.

We didn't make love. We fucked like it was necessary. Like if we didn't, something in us would break open. There was no tenderness in what we shared – just rhythm, urgency, and the quiet thrill of getting away with it.

We didn't lie to ourselves about what it was. There was no search for meaning, no posturing, no pretending it might turn into something more. There was nothing hesitant in the way we stepped into it – just the cold, thrilling truth that nothing lasts and none of this really matters.

It was never soft. Never sweet. But it was honest. And in a world full of people faking it, we at least had that.

We understood what we were doing. We chose the fire. And even now, when the smoke has long settled, a part of me still breathes it in.

My eyes finally open and I see red and fire
I'm naked and tied, exposing all
I'm wet

He approaches me slowly
Standing over seven feet
Powerful and intoxicating
Hungry and hot

Obsidian skin kissed by firelight
Horns curling like a crown of sin
Veins glowing like molten lava
And a thick, massive cock waiting for me

He wrapped a clawed hand around the base
Stroking it slowly, deliberately
Enjoying the weight of his ruinous size

"You're not built for this.
But I'll make it fit."

He grabs me with force

His claws digging deep in my sides
Using my body like a doll
Intensely thrusting in and out of me

Each thrust knocks the air from my lungs
Pain blooming into pleasure so sharp it makes me tremble
Useless against his strength, his pace, his need

"Take it.
You wanted a demon – now drown in me."

His cock splits me open with every stroke
Stretching me beyond reason, beyond mercy
My cries swallowed by flame and shadow

He slams deeper
Relentless and unyielding
The heat of him inside me – brutal, blissful, consuming

And still, he doesn't stop
He laughs, low and cruel
Dragging his tongue along my neck
Tasting fear and desire like wine

"You break so beautifully."

His claws trace down my ribs
Slow, sharp enough to sting
Blood beads
He licks it clean

He grips my throat
Not enough to stop me
Just enough to remind me I'm his
Not a lover. A plaything

Thrusting harder now
Not for pleasure, but punishment
Each movement a warning
Each sound I make, a victory

Outside the circle of fire
Shadows crawl closer
Hungry things summoned by the scent of submission

And he laughs again

Because the real torment hasn't started yet
He fucks like he's claiming a soul

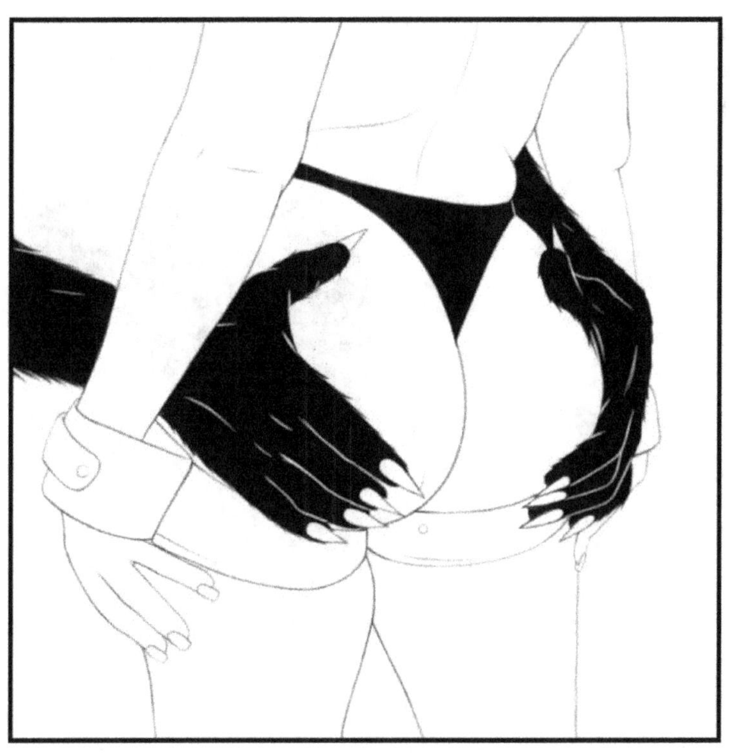

Pick Your Pleasure

You've been pulled into a dream where the rules bend. Your desire is not entirely your own. Would you rather:

Be taken by something not quite human – a presence with a voice that makes your thighs ache?

Or

Be the one who haunts, who seduces, who whispers filth into someone's ear until they beg for release?

You shouldn't be turned on by this. But your body is betraying you.

Would you rather:

Be hunted in the woods, chased barefoot and breathless – until you're caught, pinned, and claimed in the dirt?

Or

Be locked in a room where someone watches from behind the glass... until they come in and show you exactly what your moans made them do?

The Pains We Play

SADOMASOCHISM

She brought him home like a dare.

Dinner had been its own seduction – lingering forkfuls of rare steak, conversations curved with double meanings, her knee brushing his beneath the table like a challenge in silk. But he saw through the polish There was a hunger behind her charm, the kind that pulsed just beneath the skin. He's seen it before. He'd fed it before.
So, when she invited him up, he didn't hesitate.

Inside, her apartment was tasteful – intentional. Dark wood, clean lines, soft lighting. But it was the details that spoke louder. The tension in her throat when he stood close behind her. The flush beneath her collarbones. A flogger rucked behind a curtain rod, half-hidden, like she wanted to be caught.

He ran a finger along her spine before she could turn.

"I assume you're not looking for gentle," he murmured.
She shivered. "No."
Good. He didn't come for tenderness.
"Strip," he said, not loud, but absolute.

She obeyed, slowly. Not out of hesitation – out of reverence. As though each button undone was part of the ritual.

He circled her like an artist assessing a canvas. Her body was slim, toned, but not untouched. Faint marks lingered on her thighs, a faded line across her hip – poor craftsmanship from someone who lacked precision. He'd do better.

He opened his bag. She blinked at the contents – leather cuffs, clamps, a coil of jute, a short cane wrapped in worn suede.

"You keep that on you?" she asked, voice almost teasing.
He stepped closer. Gripped her jaw.
"I came prepared. Didn't you?

Her breath caught. The corners of her mouth twitched upward.

He cuffed her wrists behind her back. Tight enough to press into her skin. Not enough to cut circulation – yet.

"Safe word?"
"Crimson."
He nodded. "You won't need it."

He bent her over the kitchen island, cool marble kissing her breasts. Her breath steamed the surface. He pushed her thighs apart with his knee and stepped between them.

"Count," he said, then brought the cane down across the backs of her thighs.

"One," she gasped.
Another strike. Sharper this time. Her body arched in protest, but her moan betrayed her.
"Two."

He laid each lash with care – down her thighs, across her ass, tracing invisible lines that would swell and bruise in precise harmony. By the seventh, her voice shook. By the tenth, her legs buckled.

He pulled her upright, uncuffed her, and cupped her face, letting her lean into the warmth of his palm.

"You take pain well," he said. "But I haven't given you pain. Not yet."
She blinked, dazed. Wet.

He dragged her to the bedroom by her hair – not hard, but enough to make her follow without thought.
He had her kneel on the mattress, back arched, arms above her head. Tied them to the headboard with rough jute. Not decorative. Functional. Unforgiving.
He clipped clamps to her nipples and watched her squirm. Then attached weights, just enough to make her hiss.

"Still with me?" he asked.
'Yes," she whispered.
He smirked. "Not for long."

He slipped a gloved hand between her legs, found her soaked and pulsing. He didn't need to tease – he went in with two fingers, fast and deep, curling upward until her back bowed.
Every time she moaned, he tugged on the weights. Her pleasure became agony. Her agony, pleasure.

He fucked her with is fingers until she was sobbing.

"Please," she choked. "Please."
"Please what?"
"More. Please. Hurt me."
He smiled, dark and slow.
Then came the belt.

He left it on her skin like an oath. Across her ribs, down her back, along the curve of her ass. She screamed – once. But never crimson.

He pushed inside her without ceremony, keeping her bound, the weights still pulling, her wrists straining. Every thrust sent a ripple through the pain he'd so carefully placed on her body.

She came mid-stroke – violently, shaking, like her body didn't ask permission.
He didn't stop.
Not until she came again. And again.

Not until she collapsed, trembling and marked, against the sheets, sweat slicking her skin like a second layer.
Only then did he untie her. Wrap her in his arms.
Only then did he speak gently.

"You surprise me. You did well."
She sobbed once – then smiled though it.
"And you," she whispered, "knew exactly what I needed."

He kissed her temple.
Of course he did.

Use Me

Write about being used for someone else's pleasure. No romance. No sweet nothings. Just desire, control, and submission. How do you react when you're just a body – needed and taken.

Forgive Me, Father

He never took the collar off – not even when he had me bent over the altar.

"God sees everything," he whispered, and I swear his hands shook as he gripped my hips.

I moaned like a prayer.

The air inside the sanctuary was still – thick with candle smoke, incense, and everything we weren't supposed to do. The stained-glass casting its shimmering colors on my bare body.

I shouldn't have been there. Not like that. Not after vespers. Not after he said he couldn't see me anymore.

"This is wrong," he said against my skin, mouth trailing down my shoulder like he wanted to kiss the guilt out of me.

"Then stop."

"I didn't beg. I didn't plead. I just opened myself wider. I gave him nothing to hide behind.

And he broke – beautifully.

His hands were kind when I thought they'd be rough. His mouth blessed instead of devoured. He didn't use me. He worshipped me.

I look up at the crucifix above us, nails digging into the altar cloth, and whispered:

"Forgive me, Father... for how much I want this."

That was when he gave in completely.

He yanked my skirt higher, shoved the fabric above my waist like it offended him, like modesty was the last shred of distance between us. I felt the cool rush of air on my thighs, the heat of him behind me.

He didn't tease.

Didn't test.

He pressed the thick head of his cock against me – bare, hot, reckless – and held there, breathing like he was standing on the edge of something he could never return from.

Then he pushed in.

One brutal inch at a time.

My body clenched around him, greedy and soaked, and I heard the way he choked on a curse – how he caught it behind his teeth like it might scorch his tongue in God's house.

The wooden edge bit into my thighs. Candle wax dripped somewhere behind us, hissing as it hit stone. The scent of my sin – our sin – was thick in the air, sweat and sex mixing with incense until I couldn't tell where Heaven ended and Hell began.

He groaned like it hurt. Like it cost him something every time he pushed deeper.

"You feel like sin," he groaned.

"You feel like everything I was supposed to turn away from."

"But you didn't."

"No," he growled, thrusting deeper, hands tightening on my hips.

He set a punishing rhythm, driving into me like he needed to feel every inch of guilt – like pain would bring him closer to redemption. The slap of skin echoed through the chapel, lewd and obscene beneath the gaze of saints in stained glass.

My knees buckled. My voice rose with every thrust, every filthy grind of his hips against mine.

"I can't stop," he rasped, bending low over my back, his lips at my ear. "Tell me to stop and I will. Tell me you hate this – "

I turned my head just enough to meet his eyes, wild and ruined.

"I want more."

His hand wrapped around my throat. Not hard. Just enough to make me feel owned. One hand fisted my hair. The other slid up my stomach beneath my blouse, reverent only in how possessive he became. He touched me like he was afraid he'd be damned if he stopped.

Maybe he already was.

"I've dreamed of this," he whispered – hoarse, broken. "Heard your voice in prayer and wondered how it would sound... if you were begging."

I pressed my hips back into him, slow and shameless. I've dreamed of this.

"I'm not begging."

"You will."

And then he fucked me – louder. Rougher. With every inch, he carved his guilt deeper into my flesh.

And still, I moaned for him. For this.

Not because I wanted to be saved.

But because I wanted to take him with me.

"You should be with someone good," he whispered. "You deserve better than this."

I licked my lips.

"You feel like the only real thing I've ever wanted."

That was the last thing I said before I came – loud, raw, shuddering around him.

He didn't last long after that. He buried himself to the hilt, grinding through his release like he wanted to etch the memory into every corner of my body.

When he finally stilled, he stayed inside me.

Panting. Trembling.

His forehead rested between my shoulder blades, and I could feel the sweat dripping from his temple to my skin. The altar creaked beneath us, half-slicked with the evidence of everything we'd done.

He reached up with one trembling hand... and touched the edge of the crucifix above us.

"Forgive me," he whispered.

I turned my head, voice still thick with lust and satisfaction.

"Do you want Him to... or me?"

His eyes met mine. Ravaged. Ravenous.

"You."

They're the size of my finger, maybe smaller
Just a few inches tall
Perfect little bodies
Stiff cocks, eager mouths

I keep them in a jar
Watching them twitch and ache for me

When I tip the jar, they tumble into my palm
Sticky with anticipation
They look up at me like I'm a goddess
I am

I spread my legs
Already wet
Already hungry

I push the first one inside – slowly
His body slips between my folds
His legs kicking, arms reaching

He vanishes past my entrance
Swallowed by heat and muscle

I moan
He's squirming against my walls
Trying to brace himself as I squeeze

The next one I push in deeper
Two at once now
They press against each other inside me
Sliding against my slick, clenching flesh

I feel their cocks rubbing everything
Their hands clawing at the soft, wet ridges
They're overwhelmed
So am I

I fuck myself with them
One finger at the base, pressing them in
Holding them there while my pussy grips them tight

Every pulse of arousal shakes them
They're swimming in it
Drenched in me
Lost inside me
I can feel their screams, muffled and soaked

Their pleasure, their panic, their worship
I grind harder

I want them deeper
I want them buried so far inside they forget the world outside me ever existed

And when I come, I let it all go
My body contracts
Milking them, trapping them in the flood

I keep them until I'm finished
Until I'm dripping
Until I'm satisfied

Then I decide
Maybe I'll let them out
Maybe I'll put more in

To My Monster:

You live beneath the surface, quiet until I'm still. You stir when I am warm and open, when the soft flicker of touch turns sharp, when affection tilts into hunger. I feel you stretch inside me – slow, familiar, unashamed.

You are the part of me that wants what shouldn't be wanted. The voice that purrs when it should protest. You don't hide behind romance or permission. You are want in its rawest form – dark, unfiltered, and unbearably honest.

I used to flinch at you. I used to bite down hard on your name. But now? Now I let you speak.

Because you do not lie.

And the truth is – I like it when it's wrong. When it hurts. When it humiliates. When it strips me down to the trembling, filthy thing I am when I'm with you.

I used to try to be good. To want soft things, gentle things, things that wouldn't make me blush in the daylight. But you taught me that goodness was a cage. And I never wanted to be tame.

You press into the places I've been told to hide – the ones that ache for pain, for powerlessness, for spectacle. I let you lead me to the edge of myself, and I don't ask to come back. I spread for you. I kneel. I beg, because begging makes it worse. And worse is what I crave.

You show me what I am beneath the softness: a thing that moans at the sting, that pulses at the thought of being watched, used, punished. A thing that wants to cry and still be touched. A thing that gets wet at the word *no* – not to resist it, but to whisper *please* until it turns into *yes*.

And when it does, something inside me uncoils. Something dark and trembling and honest. I am no longer pretending to want less. I am no longer dressing my need in silence. I want to be seen – not as someone polite or pure, but as someone who asks for it. Who aches for it. Who doesn't flinch when it gets cruel but opens wider.

I want the slap and the stillness that follows. I want the sting, the stretch, the shame I don't believe in anymore. I want the danger of being known – truly known – in that hot, messy, breathless way that leaves me ruined and radiant.

So, I won't hide from you. Not anymore.

I want to be broken in beautiful ways.

I want to be taken, marked, remade.

I want every filthy thought I've ever had dragged into the light and acted out – slowly, deliberately, without mercy.

This is not a secret.

This is not regret.

This is who I am when no one's watching.

And you?

You are the only one I trust to watch – and never look away.

Room Service

We nailed the pitch. Not just "good meeting" nailed it – career-changing nailed it. The kind of win that makes people toast you with overpriced champagne and promise to remember your name.

It had been weeks of prep. Days of nerves. And now, it was over.

They gave us the suite for the weekend as a thank-you. Top floor, skyline views, and a minibar that didn't charge. I probably should've said no to a third drink, but my heels were already off, and my face hurt from smiling. I was warm and floating and more than a little drunk on relief.

I was warm and floating, tipsy on relief. The guys were in celebration mode – shirts untucked, ties slung over chair backs. Ezra had that post-win glow, all lazy grins and smug energy. Michael was quieter, grounded, always the observer – but tonight, there was a different weight in his gaze when he looked at Ezra. Something heavier. Like pride laced with want.

Back at the office, people whispered about the two of them. Nothing concrete, just shared glances, lingering pauses, that magnetic charge whenever they stood too close. No one ever knew for sure. I don't think anyone really cared.

I stretched out in the armchair while they took the couch, still reliving the best moments of the presentation, roasting each other, and half-heartedly browsing the room service menu none of us planned to use.

At some point, Ezra slid closer to Michael. Not in an obvious way – just a leg touching another, a shoulder leaning in too long. And Michael didn't move. He smiled.

I told myself not to notice. That it wasn't my business. But I watched them anyway, unable to stop analyzing the silent language between their bodies.

Then came the hush. A heavy, humming kind. Charged. I glanced at them, unsure if I was imagining it. Ezra's voice dropped. Michael's hand landed on his thigh. They weren't even looking at me anymore.

I should've said something. Broken the spell. Asked if they wanted another round of if we should call it a night.

But I didn't.

I stayed quiet. Still. Eyes flicking back to them like a guilty secret.

Then Ezra turned toward Michael – deliberate, slow – and kissed him.

It wasn't gentle. It was tentative. It was deep, open, practiced. Like something they'd done a hundred times before – just never in front of me.

And still, they didn't stop.

Michael's fingers tangled in Ezra's hair. Ezra moaned – low, hoarse – and climbed into his lap without hesitation. I gripped my glass tighter, but my throat had gone dry. My thighs clenched involuntarily. Heat pooled low in my belly.

Michael's eyes met mine for half a second.

"Are you okay over there?"

I nodded.

Ezra didn't even look back. Just grinned.

"Stay."

My heart was thudding in my chest. I watched as their mouths moved together hungrily, tongues tasting, hands wandering. They kissed like they'd missed each other. Like they were starving.

Ezra's shirt was the first to go – Michael tugged it up and off in one swift motion, pausing only to trace the exposes muscle with his fingertips. Then his mouth followed – lips brushing over collarbone, down the smooth place of his chest, circling a nipple until Ezra exhaled a broken sound.

Ezra stood, offering himself up for full view. Michael sat back, eyes trailing over every inch, then grabbed a fistful of hair and pulled his mouth along his torso – slow, claiming, worshipful.

I shifted in the chair, tension thick between my legs. I wasn't sure how long I could stay quiet, stay still. But maybe they didn't want me to.

Ezra turned his head, looking at me over his shoulder with that same dangerous smile.

"You like watching, don't you?

God, I did.

This wasn't just voyeurism – this was intimacy cracked wide open, a world I'd never been invited into… until now.

Ezra faced Michael again just as I heard the unmistakable slide of a zipper. He peeled down his jeans – slowly, teasing – revealing a hard outline beneath dark boxers. Michael's gaze stayed fixed, hungry, as Ezra stepped out of them. A show for him. A performance for me.

I leaned forward instinctively, breath shallow, drink forgotten on the side table. I expected hesitation. A glance in my direction asking for permission.

But there was none. Just desire.

Unapologetic. Sure.

Michael's hand found the space between Ezra's thighs – confident, possessive – like he already knew every sound he'd pull from him. Ezra gasped as fingers traced the outline of his cock through the cotton, slow and maddening. His hips jerked forward, needing more.

"Fuck," he whispered, head tipping back, mouth open.

Then his eyes locked on mine again – dark, heavy with heat.

Michael kissed along the inside of Ezra's thigh, tongue flicking, teeth grazing until Ezra twitched. I swallowed hard, the ache between my legs pulsing insistently.

"Don't stop," Ezra begged, voice raw.

"I wouldn't dare," Michael murmured, low and wrecked.

Without looking away from Ezra's face, he eased his boxers down, reverent. Ezra's cock sprang free – flushed, thick, leaking.

Michael stared like it was a gift. Then his tongue darted out to taste.

Ezra shuddered, knees wobbling, fingers fisting n Michael's hair as a broken moan cracked open the room.

Every motion – the slide of tongue, the hitch in breath, the subtle curve of a palm – was devastatingly erotic. It wasn't just sex. It was a ritual.

I was on fire. Aroused didn't begin to cover it. I was dripping. Desperate. My own body demanding release.

Then Michael paused, mouth still close, and he looked at me.

"Do you want to touch yourself?"

His voice was dark velvet – coaxing, commanding.

The words struck like lightning.

Before I even answered, my hand slipped beneath my dress, breath catching as heat met heat. My fingers grazed my inner thigh, then higher. The first brush over my soaked panties made me gasp – hips jerking toward my own touch.

I parted my legs wider, no longer pretending. My fingertips circled over my clit, slow, purposeful, and every nerve lit up.

They watched me – both of them. And I watched them watch me.

Ezra turned, straddling Michael now, his back pressed to that solid chest. He was fully exposed – the stunning length of him, the tension in his thighs, the wild gaze in his eyes. Every line of him bathed in shadow and heat. Michael's arm wrapped around his waist to draw him closer. Then his hand slid lower, fingers curling around Ezra's cock with practiced ease. He began to stoke him – deep and unhurried – while Ezra leaned back against him, head tilting to the side, mouth parting on a shard inhale.

They were showing me everything. And I was unraveling.

Michael's hand slid up Ezra's chest as he stroked him, each pass more deliberate, more desperate. Ezra's body responded in waves – subtle at first, then shaking with anticipation, like he was barely tethered to the moment. He was a live wire, aching to spark, and Michael was all steady hands and practiced touch.

I was a mess in my seat – legs parted, fingers slick and relentless, chasing friction like it was oxygen. The sight of them – Ezra flushed and straining, Michael solid and controlled behind him – was intoxicating. I didn't want to blink. I didn't want to miss a single breath, a single gasp, a single shift in the way they fit together like they'd done this for years in secret.

Ezra's moans were getting louder, messier. One of his hands clutched at Michael's thigh while the other curled over his own mouth, trying – failing – to muffle the sound. His body was trembling now, his hips bucking into Michael's grip, helplessly chasing the inevitable.

"Michael," he gasped, voice cracking, "I'm- "

"I know," Michael whispered into his ear, voice like smoke. "Let her see you."

Ezra's back arched, his whole body tightening like a bowstring pulled to its limit – and then he shattered. His orgasm ripped through him with a guttural cry, hot release spilling over Michael's hand, his chest heaving, mouth slack.

I couldn't breathe.

The rawness of it – the way Ezra let go so shamelessly under Michael's touch, the way Michael held him like a prize, like a lover, like something he'd earned – it pushed me right over to the edge. My own orgasm crashed over me, my fingers stuttering against the pulsing ache between my legs. I clenched around nothing, my thighs shaking, every nerve burning bright.

I didn't try to hide it. I didn't want to.

Michael kissed the back of Ezra's neck as he came down, slow and reverent, fingers still lazily stroking Ezra's softening cock. Ezra sagged back against him, chest rising and falling in uneven waves, eyes heavy-lidded and dazed.

For a moment, none of us spoke. The air was thick with heat and the scent of sex and something quieter – trust. Permission. That sacred pause where anything could happen next.

Michael finally looked up, met my gaze across the room. His mouth curved in a slow, knowing smile.

"Still with us?"

Barely.

Ezra turned his head, lips brushing against Michael's cheek as he chuckled.

"She hasn't run yet."

"Good," Michael said. His eyes didn't leave mine.

"We're just getting started."

Ezra shifted into Michael's lap, something lazy and dangerous in the movement. His gaze flicked to the still-open minibar.

"Think they stocked enough to keep us in here all night?"

Michael grinned. "We'll find out."

And then, just like that, they stood – casual, completely nude, unbothered by my stare. Ezra pulled me from the chair without warning, guiding me to my feet like I'd already said yes.

The heat hadn't left the room. If anything, it had only deepened. I felt it in the way their fingers brushed mine. In the way Ezra's mouth hovered near my ear and whispered:

"You've seen the show..."

Michael's hands trailed up my sides.

"...ready for an encore?"

But before I could answer – before anything more could unfold – Ezra leaned in, kissed my cheek, and tugged me toward the bedroom door. They didn't pull me inside.

Not yet.

They just left it open behind them.

Dreaming About It

Write a scene that lives in your subconscious. It's filthy. Maybe cruel. Maybe tender in the way only depravity can be. The kind of memory that stains your sleep and leaves your sheets damp. What happened in that dream that makes you ache in daylight?

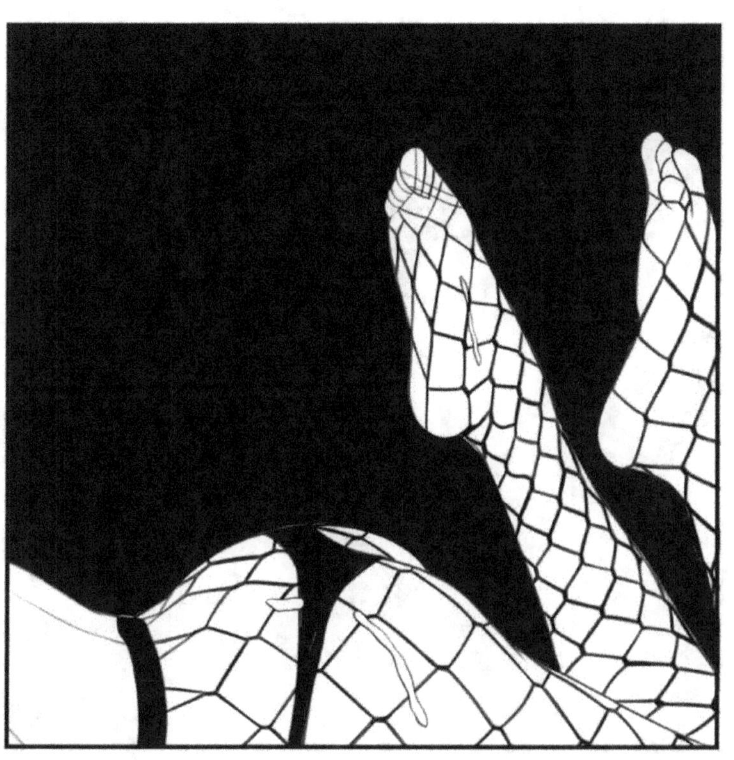

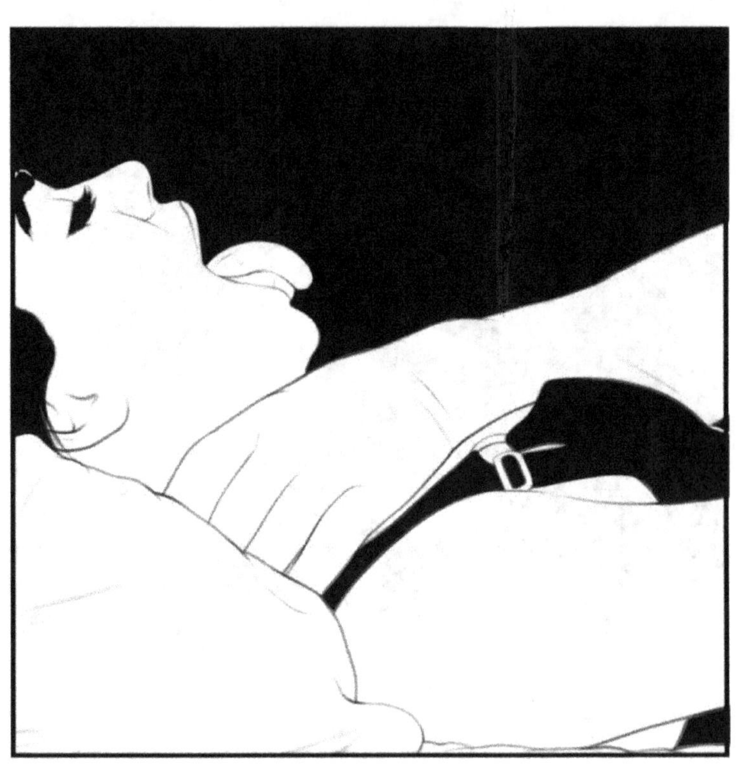

Killing Me Softly
AUTASSASSINOPHILIA

I couldn't see or hear a thing.
That was the thrill of it — the surrender, the unknown. We shared a hunger for danger, carefully measured and recklessly indulged. Our rule was simple: *no warning except one word.* "Caution." Spoken only when the scene pushes boundaries. I used to ache to hear it whispered in my ear. But I also loved how he read me — how he knew when I wanted to be pushed and when I needed to be pleased. That quiet wisdom only made me crave his punishments more. He awakened something inside me — something dark and soft and sacred. What once felt forbidden had become a kind of sanctuary.

It was Tuesday. We'd just finished a grocery run. I wore a tight, short dress — the one that always riled him up. A not-so-subtle signal that I was desperate to be touched. During the errands, I felt his stare burning through me. Hungry. Predatory. He looked at me like a beast with a full moon behind his eyes. I knew then he was ready. So was I.

As we walked to the car, he stayed a few steps behind, watching my hips sway. I gave him more to look at. I reached for the car door — and then I heard it.

"Caution."

Three seconds later, cold steel kissed the hollow of my throat.

"Get in the fucking car. Now."

A plastic bag slipped over my head, muffling my breath, and he shoved me into the backseat. I heard the trunk open. The sound of rummaging. When he returned, the blade gleamed in his hand, and he held a roll of duct tape in the other.

"I'm going to render you senseless," he said. "Do as I say, and you'll leave untouched. Disobey..." His voice dropped. His stare pinned me down harder than his knife ever could.

He bound my wrists tight. The tape bit into my skin. I couldn't touch, couldn't see. He stroked my shoulder, my neck, then grabbed my cheek through the plastic. A kiss. A slap. Then he sealed my eyes and ears with layers of tape. Darkness. Silence.
Only my mouth remained uncovered — just enough to breathe.

He got in the front seat and started to drive. The car rumbled beneath me. Every bump, every turn felt like a question mark. I lay there, helpless, adrenaline flooding every corner of me. Where were we going? What would he do? What if I disobeyed? Would he punish me with pain — or with pleasure?
When the car stopped, so did my breath.

I felt him pull me out and sling me over his shoulder, blade pressed against my backside. My legs dangled, weak. This wasn't home. I could tell by the way the ground shifted beneath his feet — loose gravel, uneven planks. Then he dropped me. Hard.

The scent of mold and rot hit me first — wet wood, stale air, something long abandoned. My pulse roared in my ears. I couldn't see him, but I knew he was there. Watching.

"You think you can tease me all day and get away with it?" His voice was low, stern, lethal. He grabbed my hair, dragging me across the floor and throwing me into a corner. My body hit the wall with a dull thud. Silence. Then — rip. My panties torn away in one brutal motion. The knife traced my thigh, cool and deliberate. A shallow cut.

One drop of blood. My breath hitched.

I was exposed. Helpless. His to command.

The blade traveled up, slicing through my top, outlining the curve of my breast. Then back to my neck, hovering above the vein that pulsed with fear and desire. I trembled beneath him, completely under his control.

And then, his hand—rough and hungry—pressed between my legs. His touch was hard, unrelenting. I gasped through the plastic, senses heightened. The contrast of pleasure and threat, the helplessness of not knowing—every nerve lit up. I was losing my mind.

"Do you want your senses back?" he asked.

I nodded – fast, frantic.

With a swift flick of the knife, he cut the bag and tape from my face. Light poured in. The sunset cast golden light through broken windows, painting him in amber. He looked feral. Ravishing. Eyes sharp with lust and something deeper — something human.

He climbed on top of me, blade still in hand. I wrapped my legs around him, pulling him closer. We kissed — hot, messy, desperate — while he pressed the knife into the floor beside my head. My wrists were still bound. He liked me that way.

This was what I craved. The not knowing. The edge. The unbearable anticipation of his next move.

"Do with me what you will," I whispered, "and pain me for your pleasure."

He spread my thighs, lining himself up. And just before entering, he paused, eyes softening. "You know I'd never put you in danger, right?"

A final reassurance. A promise. We were never reckless — we were *intentional*. There was love in the violence. Safety in the risk. Limits we respected.

And trust—the kind that let me fall apart in his hands, knowing he'd always put me back together.

Pick Your Pleasure

You agreed to the game, but the rules keep shifting.

Would you rather:

Have no safe word – no mercy – and trust they'll stop when they think you've had enough?

Or

Be taken under trance – mind hazy, thoughts slowed – so that when you wake, you only remember the ache... and the fact that you begged for more?

You've been bad. You know it. And they've come to collect.

Would you rather:

Be possessed by something dark and ancient – its voice a growl in your throat as it uses your body from the inside out?

Or

Be punished by a divine being who makes you repent with every orgasm you're denied – and every one you're forced to have?

Tastes of Temptation

There are flavors of desire only some are brave enough to taste. And I've sampled them all – each scene a different ache, a different surrender.

Praise and humiliation are where it begins – with words that kiss and cut in the same breath. *That's it, good girl,* he coos, pulling my hair while his cock fills my mouth. *So fucking pretty like this – drooling, desperate, dirty.* I melt under the praise, blush under the shame. He calls me names that make my cunt pulse and praises me until I whimper. It isn't about being degraded or adored. It's about being seen, exactly as I am – filthy, eager, and starved for both.

Breath play is the high – pure, addictive surrender. He wraps his hand around my throat like it belongs there, tight enough to steal sound but not control. My moans become choked whimpers as the edges of the world blur. Time slows. My heartbeat roars in my ears, my cunt clenches around nothing, and I float. Right when it's too much, when the stars start to bloom – he releases. Air floods in. Orgasm crashes over me. And I fall apart, reborn in the silence.

Fear play is the thrill of the unknown – a game of predator and prey with no safe word in sight. His steps echo behind me, heavy and hungry, and I know he's coming. My skin prickles. My breath catches. Then he's on me – hand over my mouth, body pressing mine into the wall. *You were told to behave*, he growls, and something wicked unfurls in me. I fight, but I want to be caught. I beg, but I don't want mercy. I want the danger – the delicious dread of being devoured.

Bondage is the stillness. Rope crisscrosses my body in tight, deliberate patterns – beautiful and brutal. I'm exposed, displayed, helpless. My arms burn. My thighs tremble. But I've never felt safer. He circles me like an artist with a brush, trailing toys, fingers, promises. My body becomes an offering, a canvas of yeses he paints with touch. I can't move – but I can feel everything. Every whimper he pulls from me becomes part of the masterpiece.

Impact play is the sting I crave when I need to be broken. The first strike lands like a kiss with teeth. Then another. And another. My ass flushes red. My thighs twitch. I count the hits and beg for more. He spanks me until I moan, then until I cry – and then until I beg for him to never stop. Every slap is a reminder that I'm real. Owned. Desired. The pain is exquisite. The release... devastating.

I don't flinch at the edge anymore – I lean into it. Every kink, every bruise, every choked breath is a reminder: I was made to be unraveled. And pleasure? Pleasure is never soft here. It's feral, filthy, and fucked into me one scene at a time.

Break Me Quietly

The bruises fade. The scratches heal. But the things whispered into your ear – the filthy, soul-staining things – they live in you.

What words wrecked you? What praise or degradation made you come harder than any touch?

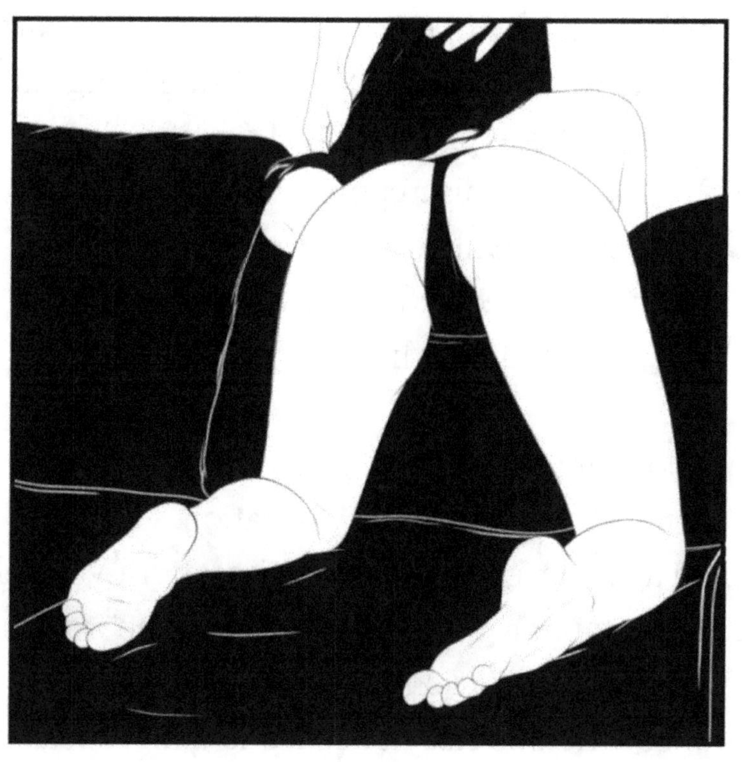

Deadline

I should've read the contract.
I mean, I did read it – the headlines, the clauses that mattered: word count, advance, royalties, the usual. It was the fine print I skimmed. The part she wrote in red ink. The part that said things like:
"Deadlines are binding. Discipline is discretionary."
"Inspiration will be extracted by any means deemed necessary."
"You may not like how this ends."

I thought it was a joke. Or a metaphor. Some twisted literary flirtation.
Then again, everything about Cassandra Vale felt like a metaphor: the way she moved, the way she looked at you like she was reading margins in your soul no one else noticed. She didn't speak in pleasantries. She spoke in commands disguised as questions.
Do you want to be good again, Adrian?
Or do you want to be great?

That was three weeks ago.
Three weeks since I handed over my ego and signed my name.
And tonight, I missed my first deadline.

The words hadn't come. Or worse – they came in pieces, dull and lifeless, like corpses I was trying to stitch into something that resembled meaning. I spent hours rearranging a single page, drinking too much wine, convincing myself tomorrow would be better.
Then, at 11:58pm, I heard the knock.

Three slow raps.
Measured. Decisive.
Not the way a friend knocks.
Not the way a stranger knocks.
No – this was a promise being collected.

My body knew it before my brain caught up. My pulse kicked. My mouth went dry. And still, I stood. Still, I opened the door.

There she was.
Cassandra.

Dark trench coat. Heels that whispered dominance across my floor. Not a hair out of place. No greeting. No smile. Just the way she looked at me – like I was a project in need of total reconstruction.

"Strip," she said.

No hello. No small talk. Just one word, spoken like a keystroke.

"I-I thought- "

Her head tilted slightly. Her gaze didn't shift.

"You thought wrong."

Silence stretched. Tension curled between my ribs, sharp and hot. I swallowed, but my hands were already on my shirt. Each button opened like a confession. I could feel the heat rise in my skin, the flush creeping up my neck – shame and arousal bleeding into each other.

I was bare by the time she took off her coat. She folded it neatly over the arm of my couch. Then she circled me. Like a predator deciding where to bite.

"You missed your deadline," she said, low and calm.
"I was trying to – "
Her fingers touched my jaw. I froze.

"No more trying. No more excuses." Her nails traced down my chest.
"You signed over control. Now, Adrian, you're going to learn what it means to surrender it."

She stepped closer. So close I could smell the leather of her gloves, the cool bite of perfume on her neck. Her voice was satin-wrapped steel.

"You don't need inspiration," she whispered. "You need correction."

Correction I –The Read & The Restraint

She didn't touch me right away.
She just watched.

I stood there, bare and stiff under her gaze, every breath embarrassingly loud in my ears. She paced once around me, slowly, like she was appraising damage.

"You used to write with hunger," she said.
"Like your hands were starving and your mouth was too proud to admit it."
Her words slipped into me like fingers under skin.
I flinched, just barely. She noticed.

"But now," she continued, circling behind me,
"you write safe. Pretty. Passionless."
A pause.
"Do you even want to be read anymore, Adrian? Or just praised?"
I swallowed, heat crawling up my spine.

She moved in closer – not touching me, but close enough for me to feel the space she occupied. Like gravity. Like command.

"I think you want to be punished for wasting your own talent. I think you want someone to take it from you. Pull it out. Force it out."

Her breath brushed my neck. I clenched my jaw, trying not to respond.

"I read your manuscript," she murmured. "Do you know what I felt?"
Silence.
"I felt bored."
That landed harder than any slap could have.
Still, I said nothing.

Because what could I say? She was right. She was always right. That's what made it worse. Better. I didn't know anymore.

"Down," she said suddenly. "On your knees."

I dropped fast – instinct more than obedience – and she tsked like she could already see the conflict bleeding through my skin.

"You're too eager," she said.
"That won't serve you here."

She walked in front of me, and I stayed kneeling, hands at my sides, the ache of arousal already starting to hum between my legs. She crossed one leg over the other, sitting on the edge of my writing desk like a queen on a throne of unfinished pages.

Then she reached into her coat and pulled out a thin, leather-bound notebook.
My notebook.
The one I thought I'd lost.
She flipped it open and began to read.

"I don't know why I can't get hard when I write anymore.
I start, I stop, I delete.
I want to be used.
I want someone to take it out of me.
Even if it hurts.
Especially if it hurts."

My breath caught. My skin went cold-hot all at once.
I hadn't meant for anyone to read that. It was a free-write. A journal. A confession I scribbled late

one night after four glasses of wine and too much silence.

But she had it.

And she was reading it to me.

She looked up, expression unreadable.

"Did you mean it?"

I hesitated. The hesitation was the answer.

She shut the notebook.

"You're not blocked," she said. "You're bloated. With ego. With fear. With the version of yourself you think you're supposed to be."

She leaned in.

"I'm going to cut it out of you."

Her hand slid beneath the desk and emerged with a thin, black velvet bag. From it, she pulled a silk blindfold, a set of leather cuffs, and a small, stainless-steel pinwheel.

My cock twitched so hard I almost whimpered.

"You'll speak when I ask," she said softly.

"You'll write when I command."

She walked behind me and knelt, one knee between mine. Her breath returned to my ear – warm, controlled.

"And if you don't?"
A pause.
"You'll learn what it costs."

The blindfold slipped over my eyes. The cuffs bound my wrists behind my back. And somewhere in that darkness, I stopped being a writer.
I became a blank page.

The blindfold was soft, but the darkness felt cruel. I could hear her move around the room. Slow. Methodical. Unhurried. The kind of stillness that made your skin crawl because you knew something was coming – you just didn't know when.

Then: the sound of metal on wood.
The pinwheel.
My body went rigid before I felt it. Then –
Prick.

Teeth, tiny and sharp, gliding across my sternum.
I gasped, breath shallow.

"Do not move," she said. "This is the foreword."

The wheel dragged downward over my nipple. It wasn't' the sharpness – it was the intention. The way she traced the outer edges before zeroing in, circling the hard, sensitive bud. I hissed. My hips flinched without permission.

She slapped the inside of my thigh.
"Still."

She continued – lower now. Down the ladder of my ribs, over the soft slope of my stomach. She was careful not to pierce. But the tension made every pass feel like I was being written on – skin turned into parchment under her edits.

"You want me to touch your cock?" she asked.
I nodded.
Another slap. This time across my stomach.
"That's not how you ask."

"...Yes, ma'am."

She leaned close. Her breath was warm on my throat.
"You haven't earned your cock yet."

Then came the vibrator.

She pressed it against the perineum – not directly on my balls, not anywhere near where I needed – and held it there. The low hum vibrated through my core, a deep, torturous pulse.
Every time I got close to the edge, she lifted it away. And waited.
I groaned.

"No noise," she said calmly. "Or we start again."

Over and over, she brought me to the brink – the kind of desperate, breathless brink where even the air felt sexual – then denied me release.

By the time she knelt in front of me and whispered, "Five hundred words. Honest ones. By tomorrow," my entire body was trembling.

I would've written in blood if she'd asked.

Correction II – The Crop & The Stretch

She didn't speak when I entered the room. No kiss. No warmth. Just command in her silence.

I was told to strip and kneel beside the desk – her desk now – while she prepared the tools. I heard the familiar swish of leather, the creak of her boots, the steady clink of buckles being tightened, adjusted. She didn't need to announce what she was doing. My body knew. My body remembered.

And then: the first sting.

The crop landed across my ass, sharp and precise. She wasn't aiming to break me – not yet. Just to correct posture. To remind me what happens when I disappoint.

Again.

Then lower. The backs of my thighs. A crueler angle this time.
My knees trembled, but she clicked her tongue and stepped in front of me.

"You miss a deadline and still expect kindness?" she asked, not waiting for an answer.
"You'll stay spread until I say otherwise. You'll thank me for every stoke."
I thanked her.
It didn't save me.

What followed was a slow, meticulous lesson in exposure. She bound my ankles to the chair legs, forcing me wide. Then she pressed two slick fingers inside me, stretching me open inch by inch until I whimpered from fullness and frustration.

"You tighten when you lie to yourself," she whispered. "You soften when you finally obey."
I moaned. She didn't stop.

The stretch turned into a rhythm. A pulse. A possession. She kept me right on the edge – hips trembling, cock hard and leaking – until I was delirious.

When I begged, she smirked and said:
“Not yet. Writers wait.”

Correction III – Use & Ruin

She let me in, then closed the door behind me without a word.
Her fingers gripped my jaw before I could kneel.
She guided me downward, rough and deliberate.

“You’re not here to think,” she said.
“You’re here to be used.”

The strap-on gleamed as she slid it through her fingers. I opened my mouth, and she filled it – slowly at first, then deeper, until I gagged and my eyes watered. She didn’t pause. She held me there. My throat worked, struggling to keep up.

The sounds were wet and obscene, echoing in the quiet room. My cock throbbed untouched, aching with every thrust.
She gripped my hair tighter.

"You'll take it," she hissed. "Because you haven't earned release. You haven't earned words."

She used my mouth like a toy, fucking it raw while tears ran down my cheeks. I gagged again. She laughed – low and satisfied – and forced my face flush against her hips.

And when she finally pulled back, letting me gasp for air, she didn't even give me time to recover. She shoved me over the desk, mounted me, and rode me with ferocity – using my body like it was hers, like my cock was hers, just another tool in her collection.

I came without permission. Loud. Shaking. Spilling across the desk like I'd been split open.

She didn't stop.

She rode me through it – overstimulation and all – until I was gasping and sobbing beneath her. A spent, ruined thing.

Then she leaned down, teeth at my throat, and whispered:
"Next time, you'll ask to come. If I say no, you'll thank me. If I say yes, you'll bleed for it."

"Don't move."

"I wasn't going to."

"You were thinking about it."

"I was thinking about you."

"That better be the only thing on your mind."

"It is. Has been since you told me to wait."

"How long have you been wet?"

"Since your first message."

"That long?"

"You talk like you already own me."

"Maybe I do."

"Then take me."

"Not yet."

"Why not?"

"Because I want you desperate. I want your voice to break when you say my name."

"Please – "

"That's not broken enough."

"Then ruin me."

"Show me. Fingers. Now."

"...Fuck – "

"Say it louder."

"It's soaked. Slipping. My legs are shaking."

"Keep going."

"I'm already so close – "

"No. Stop."

"Why?"

"Because I said so."

"You're cruel."

"And you love it."

"I do."

"Say what you want."

"I want you to bend me over and fuck the voice out of me."

"You'll scream for me?"

"I'll scream because of you."

"Then come."

"Please – "

"Now."

"Fucking – yes – "

"That's mine."

"I can't feel my legs."

"Good."

"You didn't even touch me."

"Didn't have to."

"What now?"

"Now you beg to do it again."

Beneath Wanting

What have you learned about the parts of yourself that crave – pain, power, surrender, or control? Have you feared them, denied them, or finally begun to feed them? Write, without apology, about the desires that live beneath the surface. The ones that changed you.

www.ingramcontent.com/pod-product-compliance
Lightning Source LLC
Chambersburg PA
CBHW060624310726
48982CB00003B/667

* 9 7 9 8 2 1 8 4 5 0 5 8 8 *